THE CAPTURE
(GRIFFIN TASK FORCE #3)

Melissa,
I hope you stay up
late reading this one!

[signature]

OTHER SERIES BY JULIE COULTER BELLON

THE CAPTURE

A NOVEL BY

JULIE COULTER BELLON

STONE HALL BOOKS

Cover Design by Steven Novak Illustrations
Copyright 2017

ISBN-10:0-692-88144-1
ISBN-13:978-0-692-88144-6

Printed in the United States of America
First Printing May 2017

10 9 8 7 6 5 4 3 2 1

ACKNOWLEDGMENTS

Heartfelt thanks goes to my critique partner, Annette. You make this fun.

My trusted friends and readers, Jon, Robyn, Jodi, Jeni, who have been so supportive and always make my story stronger. I couldn't do this without you. Also to my beta readers, Jewel, Marsha, and Rose, who helped me find my direction.

I am also grateful for my family who cheer me on and have given me the time to make my dreams come true. I love you!

For Brian
Thanks for helping me be brave

CHAPTER ONE

Zaya still wore the same clothes she'd worn the day she was captured, and, after all these months, they were little more than filthy rags that barely covered her. With temperatures dropping now, she'd wished countless times she'd put on something different that day. Maybe a few layers—her favorite leggings, a long-sleeved shirt and sweater, even an extra pair of socks. But, then again, that last morning of freedom had been filled with thoughts of Julian, not what clothes she might need in a wintry 6x9 cell.

She shivered and pulled the tissue-thin blanket over her shoulders. Every day the air cooled by significant degrees so she knew winter was coming on. While it was hard to be grateful for anything her captors did, she'd nearly cried when they handed the small blanket to her. Captured operatives did their best not to show emotion, but as hope of rescue leeched away from her, that had been harder to control. It didn't matter now, though. She was going to die in a cold, dark cell in central Afghanistan. The thought chilled her on the inside.

Zaya curled into a ball, trying to preserve what little body heat she had. She couldn't remember the last time she'd been warm. Well, that wasn't true. If she closed her eyes, she remembered Julian's arms wrapped tight around her, his lips on hers. The heat from his touch had blazed through her veins like wildfire. But Zaya didn't want to remember so she kept her eyes wide open, wishing the cold could numb her heart and mind as easily as it had her toes. Julian wasn't coming. There would be no rescue. This frozen rock cell was her tomb, its icy touch the last thing she would know before she died.

The clanging of the door down the hall signaled that it was time for the next meal. She drew in a breath, then wished she hadn't, as her stomach rolled even thinking about the watery bean soup and crust of bread she'd been living on. Her captors had tried to use spices and spinach to make it somewhat edible, but Zaya still had to choke it down. The smell of the spices mixed with unwashed bodies and waste made her want to retch. She pulled the blanket over her nose and breathed through her mouth to calm her stomach. Even with the revolting food and surrounding odors, she still had hunger pangs. They were a strange comfort now, a reminder that her body was functioning and could still feel.

Some days she wished she couldn't.

The small section cut out of the metal door lifted and a bowl was shoved in. If she didn't eat within the next ten minutes, the bowl would be taken away, but Zaya didn't care. She lay near the door, the food an arm's length away, but turned her back and closed her eyes. She couldn't do this anymore.

Just let me die.

The thought flitted through her mind, and she fought it for a moment. Only cowards gave up. She could stay strong until Julian found her. But even with all his resources and the Griffin Force at his disposal, he hadn't been able to do it so far. Maybe the mission to save her was destined to fail. She knew that would torment him. Julian hated to admit he couldn't do something. His drive for success was what made him the best. But with every day she spent in captivity, it looked like Nazer al-Raimi had won the battle and maybe the war. Fighting terrorism had cost her everything, and having a front-row seat to their failure was salt in the wound. It was over. She couldn't fight the inevitable. She was too tired to go on.

Closing her eyes, she finally went to the corner of her mind she rarely allowed herself to go. Laughing in the sunshine with Julian. Teasing him about the premature gray in his beard. Kissing him in their favorite coffee shop. Tears burned her eyelids. She'd never thought he'd give up looking for her, but maybe he had. How else could she explain the fact that she was still here? She pulled the blanket tighter. Being a covert operative had been her lifelong dream, but those dreams had never ended alone in a filthy cell. But, maybe it was for the best that they hadn't found her. Then they'd never know she'd stopped fighting and had given up.

It hadn't been that way at first. They'd moved her several times during her first two weeks of captivity and she'd spent her time plotting escape attempts. Each one had met with failure and beatings. That's when they'd started using drugs to keep her docile, and then she'd ultimately ended up in this basement prison. Trying to keep track of the days, she'd made markings on the wall, but when her guard found them, she'd been moved farther down the hall to this darker cell, which looked like a medieval dungeon. She'd paced her prison, exercised her body and mind, to try to stay strong. Hope had burned bright then, but eventually, with barely any food and injuries that wouldn't heal, Zaya no longer had the energy to fight. She was ready for death and hoped it came quickly.

Sighing, she turned back over and stared through the darkness at the bowl. Even with the unappetizing smell, her stomach growled, and her hand reached for it. Curling her fingers around the clay, she pulled it to her and quickly drank the liquid.

I can survive one more day, she told herself. *Hang on for just one more.*

After pushing the bowl away, she lay back down, but before she could close her eyes, the door down the hall clanked open again. Zaya's stomach sank. *Saif.* Her jailer. Her interrogator. Even in the cold air, sweat trickled down her back. He was the man who ruled her nightmares with the whip he always carried in his hand.

"Zaya," he boomed. "I've thought of more questions for you." He ran the handle of the whip across the door of her cell, his beady eyes gleaming in the light from the candle he carried in his other hand. She hated him. Loathed everything about him, from his pride at speaking fluent English to the way he enjoyed hurting others.

She sat up slowly and drew her legs underneath her. Her hand automatically went to her hair to smooth it, but instead of a familiar long braid, there were only short spikes. Saif had cut it during one of their "sessions." Rage filled her, effectively covering her helpless misery. That was why operatives were drilled constantly about compartmentalizing emotions. They didn't help in situations like this and made everything worse.

"I've told you everything." Her voice sounded weak to her own ears. She was so tired and didn't have the strength for another beating.

He opened the cell and took a step inside towering over her. If she were standing, even with her 5'8" frame, they'd be nose to nose, but he rarely allowed that. He liked to feel bigger than he was and forced everyone to sit or kneel in front of him, as if he were a king of some sort. If they refused, he put them in the box—a narrow wooden contraption that compelled the person inside into a kneeling position. Saif had left her there for hours. Her knees still had scars from her many trips to the box. But with his whip in hand, Zaya knew today's visit wasn't about feeling superior or sending her to the box. He wanted answers and would punish her to get them. The soup she'd just eaten roiled in her stomach. She couldn't endure another session with Saif. Hanging on was starting to sound like the worst idea she'd ever had.

5

The Capture

He toed her knee with his boot. "I think you need a bit more encouragement to truly tell me everything."

"There's nothing more to tell, I swear it." She backed herself against the wall. "Please. I don't know anything."

Saif chuckled, a sadistic echo that radiated prickles of dread down her spine. "But I think you do." He nodded to the guard behind him, who stepped forward to take the candlestick from Saif, who then grabbed Zaya by the arm. She knocked over the bowl trying to find her balance, but he merely dragged her behind him down the hall.

She knew the room he was taking her to like the back of her hand. A metal table was in the middle of it with restraints for her hands and feet. When she didn't answer his questions, he would whip the sensitive soles of her feet and palms of her hands. It was his specialty.

He pushed her inside and she bit back a cry of agony when her aching knees hit the concrete floor.

"Get on the table," he ordered and watched as she hauled herself to a standing position. Pain arced through her heels, still sore from their last session. Gritting her teeth, she sat on the edge of the table. She didn't have a choice. There were consequences to resisting being tied down, and it would take weeks to recover. If she did as he asked, their time together and her recovery would be shorter.

She lay down and waited while he buckled her hands and feet into the leather straps. Exposed and vulnerable, she carefully watched Saif finish making sure she couldn't move. Exhaustion and despair enveloped her. She couldn't go on like this. The tiny flicker of hope she'd felt in her cell, telling her to hang on was snuffed out as she looked at Saif, tapping his whip on his thigh.

Turning her face away, she stared at a stain on the wall. Sometimes, if she could concentrate on something else, it helped get her through the pain of Saif's "questioning" sessions.

He didn't approach her right away, but she could feel his eyes staring. "We don't have to do this, you know. Just tell me about Julian Bennet's life– the places he goes, the people he cares about– and your suffering will be over." His words were soft, deceiving. She knew what he said was a lie, but part of her wanted it to be true, if only to make the pain stop. When she didn't respond, he touched her foot with the whip handle. He used that maneuver to scare her, but today, resignation mixed with her fear, making his techniques seem more bearable.

Tell him about Julian? Did Saif want to know that Julian liked his coffee black with only a dollop of cream and no sugar? That he had a cat named Milo? No. He wanted to know about Griffin Force, Julian's resources, their black sites, and how much Julian knew about Nazer al-Raimi's network. Revealing anything would be like signing Julian's death warrant. "I've already told you. I was only a runner. I never met Julian."

The whip snapped her left foot, and she clenched her teeth. He would go easy on her at first, whipping slowly until she refused to give him the answers he wanted. Then it would get ugly.

The Capture

"I know you aren't a runner. You were seen with him." He got down in her face, his mouth twisted into a snarl. "How many operatives has he recruited for Griffin Force?"

Not enough, she thought. *Or I wouldn't still be here.*

But before she could finish that thought, an explosion rumbled through the old complex. Ceiling tiles fell on her torso, and she flinched, but with her hands and feet shackled, she couldn't protect herself.

Saif took three steps to the door and yanked it open. "Waheed!" he shouted, but his guard didn't answer. Saif shut the door again and came around to unshackle her. His fingers were clumsy as gunshots sounded outside.

Could this be the rescue she'd prayed for? If so, she needed to stall so they'd have time to find her. If it wasn't, and it was a rival terrorist cell storming the complex, she definitely wanted to be far away from here as fast as possible.

"Where are you taking me?" Zaya asked, trying to decide whether to attempt an escape. Maybe Saif also knew more than he was saying.

"You're valuable enough that I have my orders to take you directly to Nazer if anything like this happens," he said, then clenched his teeth as more ceiling tiles fell. "I need to get you out of here before this building falls down on top of us."

He grabbed her arm again and pulled her off the table. She set her foot on the floor and cried out in pain. Saif didn't slow down, and dragged her to the door. Before he could touch the handle, though, the door burst open and three men in full combat gear rushed in. Saif tried to push Zaya in front of him, but her foot was too tender, and she dropped to the floor. Everything was moving so fast, but felt like slow motion. The men were pointing guns and yelling for Saif to get on the ground. She turned her head in time to see Saif point a gun toward the tac team leader, but he didn't even have time to blink, much less pull the trigger before he was killed.

Saif's body dropped heavily to the floor next to her. *Am I dreaming?* The men's combat boots surrounded her, their voices a mix of American and British accents. *Could Julian have finally found me?*

The obvious team leader, dressed in black, leaned over her and she blinked up at him. "We're going to get you out of here, Z."

Z. No one called her that except her closest friends. Hope swelled in her chest. This had to be Griffin Force. She just couldn't place the voice yet.

He put his hands out as if he wanted to help her stand, but hesitated. "You're pretty banged up," he said carefully, looking her in the eye. "It'd probably be best if I carry you."

"We gotta get out of here," the man next to him said, touching his earpiece. "Nazer's called for reinforcements, and they're on their way." He stood next to the first man and stared down at her. "I know you're hurt, and we're going to take care of that, but we've got to get you to the helo now, or we'll lose our window."

The Capture

Zaya could only stare, her tongue thick, tears clogging the back of her throat. It was over. The nightmare was over. Nodding was all she could manage, and she didn't protest when he put her in a fireman's carry and they hustled toward the door.

From her perch over his shoulder she lifted her head to see Saif's body on the floor. Rage filled her again. His death had been so easy. No suffering. No torture or threats or prayers for death. Part of her wanted them to stop. To somehow let her mete out justice for everything he'd done to her. But it was over now, and she just wanted to be free. To go home.

Home.

A tear slipped out and blazed a trail into her hair as her rescuers rushed down the hallway of her prison. Deep down, she knew, even if they got out of there, that too much had happened for her to ever go back. Nothing would ever be the same again. Not even home.

CHAPTER TWO

Julian sat at the makeshift command center at the now-deserted Bastion Air Base. Not long ago, thousands of British soldiers had made this their base of operations, but now it was more like a ghost town, except for the team Julian had brought in. They were all holding their breath as they listened to the rescue team's radio transmissions. Augie, their computer tech, sat next to him, chewing on his thumbnail and glancing nervously at Julian every few seconds. The normally chatty computer tech knew better than to talk right now. Julian's heart was in his throat. He wanted to be there in that prison, rescuing Zaya himself, but knew he was too close to her emotionally. Letting himself near the people who had taken her would not have been a good idea. And he couldn't risk anything that would blow the mission to get her back.

The radio was pressed to his ear, though, and he strained for any information about her condition. She'd been gone six months and eighteen days. Vanished as if she'd never existed. Nazer had taunted him with the knowledge that he was holding her captive, saying that if Julian and his task force didn't back off, he'd send Julian footage of Zaya being murdered in a horrific way. Even with that threat, Julian had done everything he could to find her and, at the same time, try to stop Nazer from hurting anyone else. But every time Julian got close to bringing him down, the more he worried that Zaya would pay for this cat-and-mouse game with her life.

In the end, it was a money trail that led them to her. Julian followed all Nazer's accounts himself, meticulously picking through the transactions to shell corporations and known government officials. He'd found a financial rabbit hole that finally linked a large payment to Saif Taraki, Nazer's known enforcer. After that, it had been easy to find his whereabouts and follow him to the makeshift prison in Musa Qala, Afghanistan. Located in a desolate desert area mostly populated by native Pashtun tribes had made it harder to run covert ops, but Griffin Force had managed to get it done. When the intel came in that a female prisoner was being held there, Julian had the first glimmer of hope that they might have located Zaya.

His stomach clenched as the transmission crackled over his radio. The only words he wanted to hear were "the package is secure." But it was too soon for that. Too soon to hear anything.

"Heading for the exit point. Coming under fire," Jake's voice said, his breath coming in huffs. "Make sure Bones is waiting for us."

Something must be wrong if they were calling for Bones. That was their nickname for the team medic Elliott Burke. Zaya's injuries must be bad. The thought squeezed Julian's chest until he couldn't breathe. Part of him had expected as much, but he'd held out hope that Nazer wouldn't hurt her, that she was merely a bargaining chip. He should have known better. Nazer al-Raimi and his men had no problems hurting anyone who got in their way.

"Sir, can I get you something?" Augie asked tentatively, his fingers paused over his keyboard.

"No." Julian paced the small room, needing to burn off his anxiety. He hated feeling helpless. The months he'd spent searching for Zaya had been the worst of his life. He'd stopped sleeping for any significant length of time, reduced to closing his eyes for power naps when his body finally succumbed to exhaustion. But no matter how long he closed his eyes, the nightmares were always there– Julian running after her, hearing her scream his name, but never being able to catch up, to save her. The dreams got to be too much, so he'd lived on black coffee to stay awake as much as possible and prayed to find her.

Even with that, he knew nothing he'd gone through would compare to whatever Zaya had suffered. His mind often jumped to worst-case scenarios until he thought he'd drive himself crazy. His fists clenched. He shouldered all the blame for her capture, and he'd never be able to forgive himself for not being there. It was his new—and only—goal in life to do everything he could to earn Zaya's forgiveness.

The Capture

If they could get her out of there alive.

The radio crackled again, and he sucked in a breath. Nate, Jake, and Colt were three of the best men on Griffin Force. That's why he'd sent them after Zaya. But a small extraction team had its risks, especially when Nazer was on his home turf. He seemed to move about Afghanistan as if it were his own kingdom. Stealing Zaya back would be a huge coup, and Nazer would most likely come after them even harder if they succeeded. Julian couldn't care about any of that. He just needed the words that she was safe.

He pressed the radio to his ear, not wanting to miss any part of the incoming transmission.

"Package is secure."

It took a moment for the words to sink in. Had he dreamed them? But then they finally registered. Zaya was on the helo. Safe. He sagged against the wall, finally slumping to the ground, unable to stand the mountain of relief pouring over him.

"Your plan worked! They got her out." Augie slid down the wall next to Julian, pointing at the blue plaid shirt he loved to wear when they were on ops. "Commander, I'm telling you, every time I wear this shirt, the mission ends in success."

"Never take it off." Julian could hardly speak. His mind was racing ahead. Getting Zaya back would only be the beginning. Dealing with what had happened would take a lifetime. What had she been forced to endure? Could she come back from it?

Suddenly the air in the command center was stifling. He had to get out. After pulling himself up, he jerked open the door. The air outside wasn't any more breathable—its dryness made his throat itch—but he sucked in a few breaths anyway and tilted his face skyward. It was too early for any sign of the rescue helo, so all he got was a faceful of sun. Temperatures had been more comfortable with winter coming, but the days could still be hot. He wouldn't be sad to leave Afghanistan behind.

Thinking back, his last day with Zaya had been warm and bright like today– and full of so much hope. Late spring in Morocco was beautiful, and when he knew he'd be there with Zaya, he'd contacted his jeweler friend, Nabil—not because he would help with their assignment, but because Julian was ready to choose an engagement ring for Zaya. They'd been discussing marriage, and Julian was planning the perfect proposal. The Moroccan mission was supposed to have been a quick pickup of one of Nazer's associates to take him to a black site for questioning, so there should have been plenty of time to pick out a ring. They should have been to Morocco and back within seventy-two hours, but Julian hadn't considered the idea the pickup was a trap. He'd been too preoccupied with the ring, how he would propose, and what her answer would be.

Their last movements together that day ran through his mind on a loop as they had thousands of times before. That last morning when they'd left the hotel, on their way to the counter-terrorism facility where Nazer's associate Mbarek Bahnini was being held. Laughing and chatting about the little man on the sidewalk who'd tried to cheat them out of eighty dirhams to be their "tour guide." Julian had held her close, glad she was his to love, and excited to make his proposal.

They'd been a little bit early to the counter-terrorism facility, but it hadn't taken long before Bahnini was brought out of the holding cell and secured in the transport vehicle. Julian told Zaya he'd meet her at the airport since Nabil's jewelry shop was five minutes away, and he wanted to have her ring in his pocket before they got on the plane. Zaya had raised an eyebrow, but smothered her curiosity, just nodding. Looking at her trusting, beautiful face, he'd wanted to drop to one knee and ask her right then, but there was no way he would have lived down the utter lack of romance by proposing marriage to her in front of a Moroccan counter-terrorism office. Instead, he'd kissed her goodbye and watched her get into the back of the van.

That was the last time he'd seen her.

As near as he could guess, the motorcade had been attacked at the same moment he'd put her emerald engagement ring in his pocket. He'd been on his way to the airport in a little blue taxi when he saw the smoke just ahead. Blindly, he'd jumped out and ran for the scene. Bloody carnage everywhere. No one had been spared. Their prisoner was shot execution-style, still handcuffed in the back of the van. The driver and first guard were obviously dead, but the second guard from the back of the van had been lying half in and half out of the door. When Julian approached, he'd still been alive. Julian held his head, knowing from the rattling breaths, he didn't have much longer.

"Zaya?" Julian had asked, praying she wasn't dead.

"Taken," the man had whispered. "Nazer."

It was a small relief, but those two words shook him to his core. From that moment on, the ring box in Julian's pocket was like a cannonball of regret. There was no doubt Nazer had been after him, as the head of Griffin Force, and Julian would have been there if not for the ring. Instead, one of the most wanted terrorists in the world had gotten Zaya. The guilt was crushing.

Julian had been driven in his hunt for Nazer before, but from that day on, he was relentless. He called in every favor he was owed and used every penny at his disposal to find Zaya.

And now he had.

It was impossible to stand still. He strode back and opened the door to the communications building he'd exited. Augie was at the computer, monitoring the helo. Judging from the little blip on the screen, Zaya was about ten minutes out and they had the all clear. Good.

"I'm going down to the landing zone," Julian said to Augie, pushing down his jitters. After all these months of waiting, Julian needed to make sure he was there the moment she touched down. Augie nodded absently, and Julian walked away. Several Griffin Force soldiers who were guarding the perimeter eyed him as he passed by, but no one approached. He was glad. Explanations, or small talk, were beyond him right now.

The Capture

Camp Bastion had a lot of empty space, but as soon as he'd received the go ahead to use the buildings on the far edge of the camp, the first thing he'd done was secure a makeshift airstrip. His steps slowed, and he began to pace the length of the landing zone, waiting for the helo. Finally, he heard it. Shading his eyes, he watched the descent. Sand briefly obscured the aircraft as it landed, and Julian took a step forward, letting the rushing granules sting his face, reminding him that this was real. She was here. His stomach was in knots as he waited for the aircraft to be safe for approach, and then he was running, needing to see her.

The helo door opened, and Jake Williams, still in tactical gear, put up his hand. "Wait. Give her a minute."

But Julian had waited six long months. He pushed Jake to the side and climbed aboard. Elliott was there in the middle of the floor, his entire focus on the woman lying very still before him. A woman that looked nothing like the Zaya he remembered.

Her long, brown hair was now short and matted. She looked filthy, but underneath the dirt, it was obvious her skin was pale and waxy-looking, as if death had claim on her, but hadn't quite received its due. Her cheekbones were more prominent than they had been six months ago, and her one visible wrist was bruised and looked like it could be snapped in two with only a touch. His heart wrenched hard, twisting his insides and making it difficult to breathe.

He looked at Elliott, whose eyes were full of compassion. "Y-you probably have a lot of questions, but r-right now we need to get her inside," he said just loud enough for Julian to hear. "She needs t-treatment for an infection in her foot."

"Her foot?" Julian held on to the edge of the door, trying to steady himself. Standing there, frozen in place, wasn't how he imagined their reunion. He wanted to be strong, to be able to comfort her, but it was as if his body could only stare dumbly and try to process the scene in front of him.

"Some d-deep lacerations that haven't h-healed properly. She's got a f-fever, and we need to get that under c-control." His tone was brisk as he started to move the stretcher into position for transport. "Once she's s-settled, we can t-talk about where to go from here."

Julian nodded. That was reasonable. But he didn't feel reasonable. He wanted to take her in his arms. To tell her how sorry he was. To beg her to forgive him for sending her in the van alone. Instead, he stepped back and watched as they lowered the stretcher from the helo. She didn't move. Was she unconscious? Sleeping?

As if Zaya had heard his unspoken question, she opened her eyes, squinting at the sun. Julian leaned over and took her hand carefully in his, feeling the raised skin of scars on her palms. What had they done to her?

"Z, it's me, Julian."

For one brief moment, she squeezed his hand and brought it to her cheek. But then her brown eyes locked on his, and he couldn't hide his shock at her obvious pain and misery. His breath seized at how naked and raw the emotions swirling between them were.

"I'm sorry," he murmured, not knowing what else to say, but needing to say something and hear her voice. "So very sorry."

She gave a slight shake to her head, then turned away without a word, her light tugging on his hand forcing him to release her.

"We've g-got to treat her now," Elliott said, as they moved her into the triage area. "You'll have t-time to talk later."

Julian folded his arms and watched them take her into the hospital, trying to calm the feelings inside him. It felt as if his soul had been raked over the coals, the hot trail of guilt and regret leaving a path that burned through his body. The agony of being separated from her had multiplied at seeing the result of her captivity. And from her reaction, she blamed him, just as he blamed himself.

He started toward the hospital, but quickly detoured back to the command center where he'd spent the morning waiting for news. He wrenched open the door. Augie was inside, engrossed in whatever was on his computer screen. He glanced over to see who'd come in, a puzzled look on his face.

Julian managed to get eight words, "I need to be alone for a minute," past the lump in his throat. Augie didn't ask any questions, just closed his laptop and scurried past him immediately.

Once Julian was alone, he locked the door and slid to the floor again, his head in his hands. A groan escaped from deep inside, and, after that, he couldn't stop the anguish flooding over him like an avalanche. Silent tears coursed down his face. He knew he would need to be strong for Z in the days ahead, but he needed a window of time to mourn for what she'd suffered and the fact that nothing would ever be the same again. For either of them.

He didn't know how long he sat like that, but a knock at the door and Augie's plaintive voice jolted him back to the present.

"Sir? Sir, you're needed at the hospital. They're calling for you to come immediately." He was agitated, more so than usual. That meant trouble.

Julian scrambled to his feet. The only reason the hospital would call was if something had happened to Zaya. Remembering how fragile she'd looked, alarm raced through him.

"On my way," he said, as he pulled the door open. She wasn't going to die now. Not if he had anything to say about it.

CHAPTER THREE

Zaya was surprised she'd been able to sleep after her rescue, but being surrounded by armed men she trusted to protect her, combined with the soothing *thwump thwump* of the helo rotors as they'd flown to safety, had lulled her into a deep and dreamless sleep. Energy was starting to creep back into her veins as she lay on the gurney. She'd never liked the smell of hospitals, but that crisp, clean smell was welcome now. The men who'd brought her in were congregating outside the door and she could hear the murmur of their voices. Was Julian out there? She closed her eyes. He'd looked haunted when he'd touched her hand, and his eyes were so full of shock, then pity. She felt ugly and broken, and couldn't bear to see that confirmed in his face, so she'd turned away.

Lost in thought, the lights above her went out and she was startled when a hand grabbed her ankle. Instinctively she sat up, adrenaline shooting through her. A voice came through the darkness, telling her it would be all right, but she couldn't concentrate on his words. The darkness. The hands on her feet. She was back in prison. *Saif!* Her subconscious was screaming to protect herself.

The overhead lights flickered back on, and she grabbed the first thing she saw that could be used as a weapon. Jumping off the bed, she crouched as best she could, battle-ready, a scalpel in hand. Her heart was racing, but it felt good to finally have a weapon to defend herself. She looked up, expecting to see Saif's familiar scowl, but it was a doctor in green scrubs and a white coat. Her fingers twitched on the scalpel, knowing she should put it down, but her body wouldn't respond to commands. All she could think was she'd never let anyone near her again. No one would touch her without her permission.

The doctor reached out, palms up, but she backed up against the small counter. The need to flee was overwhelming.

"Stay away," she shouted, but her voice was little more than a croak.

The long empty room had several beds on one side and a trauma area on the other. The only exits were at either end. Zaya inched toward the one closest to her.

"We want to help you, Zaya," the doctor said, his tone even and soft, as if she were a frightened child. "Put that down and we can talk."

"I can't. I don't want to." Her voice was so hoarse and she was desperately thirsty. And cold. The fever was giving her chills, but she'd been cold for so long, it sort of felt normal. "I have to get out of here." She shifted to face him and familiar pain shot through her feet and radiated up her legs. She ignored it. The freedom beyond the closed doors beckoned to her.

The doctor nodded to the men watching them from the window in the door. They moved away. "I get that you don't know me. There are a lot of unfamiliar faces here. But all we want to do is help you." He glanced down at her feet. "You need to be treated."

As if coming out of a fog, his words made sense and Zaya could see the situation clearly. She lowered her arm, but a nurse burst in behind him and panic rushed through her again. The scalpel automatically flicked toward the nurse and Zaya knew she had to get out there if she didn't want to hurt anyone. "I'm leaving. I need to go."

"What's going on here?" A voice boomed from the direction of the door where the other men had been, and within another second, Julian appeared and stood next to the doctor. He looked so strong and capable standing there, it took her breath away. She wanted to lean on his strength, but with a shaking scalpel in hand, and her body's reactions so unpredictable, she didn't dare let him close. Zaya had spent months compartmentalizing her feelings and memories of Julian in the corners of her mind. She called on that ability now, blanking everything from her mind.

He took in the situation with a glance, then stepped toward her. Too close. She backed away.

"Don't." She lowered the scalpel. "I'm not . . . I'm not myself. I don't want to hurt anyone. I need to leave." She was mumbling and unsure if anyone even heard her. Taking a tentative step toward the far door at the opposite end of the room, she stumbled. Julian reached out, but she shrank back. "No."

"Z, let me help you. Please."

She dared to look up at him. The crease in his brow said he was unsure how to respond to her. She was feeling the same way. What was the appropriate response when someone you once loved returned from captivity?

"I don't know if I can." She set the scalpel on the counter behind her, taking a deep breath to lower her heart rate.

Julian took another step toward her. She looked at his clenched jaw, at the beard he'd grown since she'd last seen him. He looked more hardened than she remembered. His eyes were shadowed now and his expression was wary, as if he couldn't read her either. But just having him here was oddly soothing. She'd dreamed of it for so long, yet, in all her dreams she'd never held a weapon on him. The thought made her take another step back, needing some distance between them still.

He didn't seem perturbed by that, his eyes staying focused on her face. "This is Dr. Hixsom," he said, pointing in the general direction of the doctor. "Z, we just want to get your wounds taken care of and some antibiotics in you. Maybe get rid of your fever and find you something to eat, okay? One step at a time."

Zaya dropped her gaze to the floor as the panic ebbed away. Tears welled in her eyes, and she didn't want him to see them. Instead, she merely nodded and moved back toward the bed.

The nurse in the corner of the room inched slowly toward her, and Zaya noticed she carried a covered food tray. "You must be hungry," the nurse said quietly. "Maybe you could eat something while you're getting fixed up."

Now that Z was aware of the tray, she could smell the tomato soup. Her mouth watered. It had been too long since she'd eaten anything but bug-infested liquid that couldn't even be termed broth. For a moment, the entire room narrowed down to that soup and how badly she wanted it. Zaya forced down the urge to grab it out of the nurse's hands and devour it. She locked her joints and stayed where she was. Could she eat like a civilized human being when she was ravenous? She didn't know. What if she embarrassed herself in front of everyone in this room? Julian's eyes were still on her, she could feel it.

"I want . . . I . . . Can we clear the room, please? I'd like to talk to the doctor alone." She raised her chin and willed her tears away. If she looked strong enough, maybe Julian would step outside. He was the last person she wanted to witness her first meal out of captivity.

He stood there, tense and silent, as if her words had rooted him to his spot. Finally he said, "That's fine. I'll wait in the hallway." But he didn't back away. Instead, he reached out for her, his hand suspended in the air. She stared at it, but couldn't meet him halfway. "No one's going to hurt you here, Z. I promise."

The Capture

"I stopped believing in people's promises a long time ago." She winced at the abruptness of her words, but straightened her spine. He couldn't look at her again with love, not after what had happened. All she would ever be now is his rescue project and she didn't want that.

His hand still reached out to her, waiting for her to take it. It was symbolic, in a weird way. His hand was outstretched, his help being offered, but she didn't know if she'd ever be able to take either one. Raising her eyes, she searched his face. He must see her as the shattered version of the woman she'd been.

"I'll keep you safe, Z." His voice was soft, the words for her ears alone.

She closed her eyes. "There's nothing to save anymore, Julian." She felt dead inside. He'd realize that soon enough. She flinched when he moved close enough to lightly touch her shoulder and turned her back to him. A small shiver went down her arm, the same reaction she'd had to him from the moment they'd met. She pulled away, hoping he hadn't felt any acknowledgment from her, and lay down on the bed. Her body felt like it weighed two tons, and she was tired. Exhausted. "I'd like to be alone with the doctor now."

"I'll come back in a bit to start your debrief," Julian said, and her eyes flew to his.

"No. Not you. Not now." Zaya sat up quickly and swayed with dizziness. She clutched the bed railing to steady herself. She couldn't tell him what she'd been through these last months. The questioning. Beatings. The hope. Despair. Those details were hers to deal with alone. Julian wouldn't understand what she'd been through, and there was no way she was going to let herself be some pity case for him. Ever.

"We can talk more after you've had a chance to eat." He backed away, but when her mind registered he really was leaving, the more she wanted to ask him to stay. Everything was so confusing, as if her mind couldn't make up what it wanted. Pushing him away seemed logical. She didn't want him to see what she'd become, to know what she'd been forced to live through. But a small piece of her heart wanted to go back to how it had been before all of that. For a second, looking into his familiar brown eyes, the smallest sliver of hope opened up inside her, but she slammed that door shut. She couldn't go back.

She watched the nurse setting up the tray on a rollaway table next to her. "Find someone else from the team to debrief me."

He clenched his fists and closed his eyes. "Z, I need to hear it, okay? I need to know. I . . . Please, don't shut me out."

She didn't answer, struck by the anguish in his voice. Telling him would magnify that pain. For both of them. Couldn't he see that?

When he finally opened his eyes, the hurt had been pushed back, and the determined look she'd been well acquainted with was in place. He kept his word, though, and retreated to the hallway without saying anything else.

She watched him leave, her head throbbing as she tried to sort through all the feelings churning inside her. *What should I do?* Telling him would hurt him. Not telling him would hurt him. And she didn't feel like herself. The doctor was approaching her cautiously, as if afraid she'd strike out at him or something. Everything was off.

"Would you like to eat first or take care of the wounds on your foot?" The doctor's eyes were watchful, the same way soldiers were when they were in the middle of a mission.

Keep your eyes open, notice the details because the threats come where you least expect it. How many times had that been drilled into her when she was on active duty? But was she a threat to those around her?

She pushed her hunger pangs away. "Let's get my feet taken care of first," she said with determination. "Then maybe I can eat without the pain throbbing up my legs."

With that thought, all the fight went out of her, and she lay back on the bed while the doctor prepared to stitch up her foot. She'd been alone in that cell for so long; maybe isolation was the best thing for her. To be alone, hidden from normal people. Tears pricked her throat.

She swallowed. If she was going to have a chance of ever being normal again, she had to relearn how to interact with people. Starting with the doctor. "I'm sorry," she said, watching Dr. Hixsom pull on surgical gloves. "This is going to seem weird, but I need you to tell me exactly what you're doing before you do it, okay?"

"That's not weird at all." He seemed to relax at her words and sat on a little stool before he pulled a tiny table of gauze and medical instruments close. "You've been through a traumatic experience. I understand that, and I'm going to do whatever I can to help you fix the outer damage." He leaned in a bit, his blue eyes clear and kind, completely opposite of the other men she'd seen in the last six months. "It's going to be up to you to fix yourself inside, though."

Zaya let out a breath. She didn't answer, but she knew he was right. She also knew there was a lot of work to do on that front and a chance she couldn't ever heal fully.

Her stomach rumbled so loud and hard, she put her hand over it. "Do you mind if I have the soup while you work?" She didn't wait for the doctor's permission and pulled the food tray close.

The doctor nodded and she watched as he and nurse worked in tandem to clean the fresh wounds on her feet. It was relaxing, in a way. Or maybe the relaxation came because she was actually eating something warm, with flavor. It was hard to take small sips, though, and not gulp the whole bowl.

When they were done, she pushed her empty bowl to the side. "I'd like to take a shower and change my clothes."

"We need to keep these stitches clean, so a sponge bath will have to do," the doctor quietly said as the nurse cleaned up. Zaya wiggled her toes. For the first time in months, she didn't have any pain in her feet. The numbing medicine the nurse had applied to her soles had been the single best thing that had happened to her all day. Second only to the food.

"The nurse will bring you some clean hospital scrubs, though," he added.

"Thanks." Clean clothes sounded like the closest thing to heaven at the moment, even if they were scrubs. Zaya wondered if Dr. Hixsom had ever taken a change of clothes for granted. He looked very clean and put together, as if he weren't in the middle of Afghanistan where sand found its way into every nook and cranny.

It didn't take long before the nurse reappeared with a small portable basin and helped shampoo her hair. Then, she pulled the curtains shut and Zaya was left alone to bathe and get dressed. She couldn't stop sniffing the new scrubs. It had been so long since she'd smelled something clean, even if it was a little antiseptic.

She reached up to touch what was left of her hair. After several washes, it finally felt clean, but it was woefully uneven, and the ends barely touched below her ears. A little sob welled in her, remembering Saif and the sound of the shears as he'd cut her long, beautiful hair, promising to stop if she'd just give him the information he wanted. She pressed her hand to her mouth. There would be time for crying later, when she was far away from anyone who'd known her before, including Julian.

As if conjured by her thoughts, Julian slowly pulled the curtain back and gave her a smile that was big enough to show his dimple. "Feeling better?" Julian asked, his broad shoulders filling the smaller doorway. He'd also bathed and was clean-shaven, making it easier to see his cleft chin. That little indent had been her favorite place to touch on his face, right before she pulled him down to kiss her. She shivered at the thought.

"Much better." She folded her arms over her middle. Would she ever stop having a physical reaction to this man's presence? She kept her eyes on his face, not wanting to notice how the rest of him looked in his t-shirt and cammies. He'd always been too handsome for his own good, and though he was thinner now, he still took her breath away.

As if he knew her resistance was weak, he stood next to her bed, close enough she could feel his body heat. She scooted away a half an inch. The scene with the scalpel was too fresh in her mind and she couldn't trust herself just yet.

"I need to ask you a few questions." His voice was low and controlled, as if he were afraid to ask her anything. Or was it the answers he feared?

She couldn't be near him, answer his questions, see his pity. "I need some time, Julian, and I'm so tired. Can we save this debrief discussion for tomorrow?"

Knowing what Nazer and his men had done to her would ratchet up his guilt and there wasn't anything he could do about the past. Besides, talking to him about what had happened was too hard to do when she was so emotional. When she was finally debriefed by someone, she wanted to be able to be detached. That definitely wasn't something she could achieve today. She looked up at him, unblinking. Surely he wouldn't deny her a reprieve?

The Capture

His eyes roamed over her face, as though he was trying to reconcile the woman he'd known with the one right in front of him. She turned away and ducked her head, feeling self-conscious. It was probably hard for him to even recognize her with how hideous she looked.

He softly touched her cheek with one finger, putting barely enough pressure on it to turn her face and meet his eyes. The moment filled her with so many memories of him, his love, and his kisses, it was as if the compartment in her mind had spilled over.

"Don't turn away. You don't have to hide," he murmured, staring down at her.

"I'm not the same, Julian. They . . ." Her throat constricted, as if her body didn't want to give voice to her fears. "They cut my hair. I . . . I feel ugly."

He brushed a spiky tendril away from her face, letting his fingers run through it and linger at the end. Longing shot through her. She'd ached for him for so long and now he was here.

His hand fell away, but he held her gaze. "You're beautiful. Long hair or short, you never have to wonder about that."

She closed her eyes and shook her head. "Don't say that. It's not true." Daring to look up at him, the tenderness in his face pulled her in and awareness arced between them. She let herself feel it for just a moment, her heart skipping a beat as his eyes dipped to her lips, before she moved away. Even though she still cared what he thought, there was so much she still had to process, it was best if she kept her distance.

"I wouldn't lie to you about that." Julian drew in a long breath, clearly not unaffected by their closeness. He gave her a quick glance before he went to the small table near her bed, and grabbed a water bottle.

"Sorry, it's not very cold, but it's liquid and you should stay hydrated." He handed it to her, then leaned against the bottom of the bed. "We don't have to talk specifically about the details right now, but could you give me some preliminaries? Like anything you remember about locations you were held? We've shut down all of Nazer's training camps and his base of operations, and we're pretty sure the prison you were in was his last stronghold. That is, unless you can think of somewhere else," he said finally.

All her warm feelings toward him iced over immediately and her jaw dropped in surprise. All he'd been thinking about was shutting down Nazer's stronghold? She was just a means to an end? Hot anger slid down her spine and her fists clenched. "Is that why you left me there for months? Because you were busy shutting down Nazer?"

"Of course not," he snapped. He ran a hand through his hair and backed up a step. "On second thought, maybe we should just talk tomorrow."

She swung her legs over the side of the bed, her outrage giving her energy. "Was I some sort of bait to see where Nazer would take me to next? Then you moved in and shut it down when they transferred me somewhere else? I guess I was lucky you rescued me at all." Her hands were shaking, and she twisted them in her lap.

"No." He shook his head for emphasis. "We found Nazer's hideouts, the people who sheltered him, his hidden family members, all *while* we were looking for you. But all of that was the *indirect result* of looking for you. Secondary." He moved closer again and looked like he was going to reach for her hand, but thought the better of it and pulled back. "I swear it."

She stared at his face. Once, Zaya had known him as well as she'd known herself, and looking into his eyes now, she could see he was telling the truth. As fast as the anger came, it melted away, leaving her open and defenseless. "Why did it take so long?" The words slipped out before she could stop them, barely more than a whisper.

"You were spirited out of Morocco within twenty-four hours. It took me weeks to figure out you were in Afghanistan." The pain in his voice was unmistakable. "You know how many hideouts Nazer had worldwide. I searched every one, praying you could hold on."

"I prayed you'd come." She dug her nails into her palms, feeling the scars from the whip. "During every beating, I held out hope that that day would be the one where you'd rescue me." Zaya turned her face away, feeling a tear trickle down her cheek.

Before she could protest, Julian gently pulled her into his arms and held her against his chest. She felt her body

36

involuntarily stiffen at the surprise contact and she forced herself to relax by closing her eyes, taking a deep breath, and letting herself be close to him for a moment. It had been so long since anyone had hugged or held her.

"I'm sorry," he said into her hair. "You have no idea how sorry I wasn't there to protect you."

It has been six months since she'd been in his arms and her memories of how brilliant his embrace was had been accurate. "I've wondered for so long where you went that day. Why did I have to meet you at the airport?"

His arms tightened around her briefly, and he hesitated a bit too long before he said, "It's a long story."

"I've got time." She tried to pull back and look into his face, but he held her fast.

"I want to tell you, but not here, not like this." He let his hand brush the nape of her neck. "You've been through enough."

His voice sounded resigned, as if whatever he was going to say would hurt her. She'd run the scenario through her head again and again and couldn't imagine where he'd gone that last day. *Meet me at the airport*, he'd said, but why? Where had he gone, and why couldn't he tell her? They'd told each other everything, and, back then, were in such a good place. It had seemed like marriage was the next step and Zaya had even let herself dream about being Julian's wife, but he'd started acting a little weird and sort of secretive in Morocco. Maybe the talk of marriage had scared him off, and he'd been planning to break up with her. If that was the case, seeing her now would make it crystal clear that she wasn't meant to be anyone's wife, especially his. Her body and soul were beyond damaged. Scarred. Too broken, especially for someone like Julian, who was larger than life.

She used all her energy to push away from him. He eased back, but stayed close. "Never mind. None of it matters now."

"What do you mean?"

She bit her lip, knowing it had to be said. Out loud. "Everything's different. We can't go back, Julian. Surely you know that."

He sighed. "I *don't* know that. Neither of us does. But no matter what happens between us, at least let me help you recover."

Have him hovering over her with his secrets? With his pity, guilt and regret? Never. "Thanks, but I think I'll be fine on my own."

"You always were stubborn." He reached out and touched her hair, as if reassuring himself that she was really in front of him. "Dr. Hixsom is running some tests and the results won't be back until tomorrow. So I have about twenty-four hours to convince you to let me help." He playfully tugged on the piece of hair near her earlobe.

The familiar gesture used to bring a smile to her face, but now tears were close to the surface. He'd always loved playing with her hair, especially when she had braids or a ponytail, but now, there wasn't much hair left at all. Could she trust what he'd said about her appearance?

"Don't be too sure," she said, sadly. She stared, unblinking, hoping her emotion wouldn't be noticeable.

"I'm not going to pressure you, Z, but I want you to see you're not alone. That you can still trust us. Me."

"I can't," she said, not meeting his gaze. "You don't know . . . " her voice trailed off. How could she ever explain?

He briefly touched her hand, then headed for the door. "It's been a long day. Get some sleep, and we'll talk more tomorrow."

He reached to turn off the overhead lights, but a ball of panic made her shout out. "No!"

Julian turned and Zaya could feel a flush staining her cheeks at the startled look on his face. "I mean, could you leave the light on, please?" She fiddled with her blankets, not meeting his stare. She'd been in the dark so long; she needed light.

"Okay." Indecision flitted across his face as he took a step toward her.

Zaya rubbed her hand across her face, willing the telltale redness to go away. How embarrassing to show Julian how weak she really was. Thankfully, he changed his mind about approaching her again and moved toward the door. "See you tomorrow."

She watched him leave, then turned on her side. Their history complicated everything, made her feel what she wasn't ready to face yet—that she still had feelings for him, but couldn't be the woman he needed. His pained apology when she'd first seen him also told her he had some misplaced guilt, but he'd have to find his redemption some other way. The only merciful solution for both of them was to make sure there weren't constant reminders of what they'd lost, and leave before he came back in the morning.

After spending months hatching escape plans from whatever dark hold or dirty cell Nazer had put her in, it was easy to make the decision to at least calculate her options here. She sat up and looked around the long, narrow room. There weren't a lot of easy and undetectable choices for getting off of an airbase, but there were a couple. She'd definitely need a vehicle since she couldn't walk far, but it would be nearly as difficult to drive with the condition of her feet. She had to try. Making her own decisions now was the first steps in getting her life back.

And she would have to do it by leaving the only man she'd ever loved.

CHAPTER FOUR

Julian sat in the hall, wishing now he'd thought of getting Zaya treated in a different location. In his mind, Camp Bastion was a good stopover point on their way out of Afghanistan, with the facilities needed to triage her injuries. But with the overwhelming need to protect her at the forefront of his mind, the nearly empty hospital feel exposed and too open. The deserted camp buildings still stood as sentinels in the desert from when the British had occupied them, but now he wished he had some of the thousands of soldiers that used to live here available to keep Zaya safe.

He ran a hand over his face. Maybe he was projecting his own vulnerabilities onto the mission, since nothing had gone as planned once she'd been freed. He couldn't shut off his raw and jumbled emotions, which was something he'd never experienced in the field before. But this was more than a hostage rescue and Zaya was more than just another mission. She was everything to him.

Julian stared at the door to the examination room. Her plea to leave the light on had lanced through him. He'd wanted to go to her, to hold her and fight off the demons she was now fighting alone, but it was easy to see she wasn't in a place to allow it yet. Obviously, she blamed him and didn't want him close. Hard to take, but he understood it. He clenched and unclenched his fists, trying to separate his feelings from the mission. Getting her safely home to England was the primary objective, but helping her cope with her new reality was his personal priority. Balancing it all was proving more difficult than he'd thought.

Letting out a breath, he sat back in his chair. Julian could still hear the soft murmur of the two nurses down the hall as everyone settled in for the night. Neither of them had batted an eyelash when he said he wanted to stay near her room. He'd talked about safety reasons, but in truth, he just wanted to be close, as close as Zaya would allow. If that meant being uncomfortable all night in the hallway, that's what he'd do.

He folded his arms, his eyelids heavy. After so many months of having his every waking moment focused on finding her, it was hard to wrap his brain around the fact that she was found. She was safe and in the next room. And he was going to make sure she stayed that way.

He let his chin fall to his chest and closed his eyes. It felt good to have her close, like he could finally breathe again. And with nothing but the half-darkness of the hallway to witness it, he finally let himself sleep.

After what seemed like only a few minutes, Julian felt a hand on his shoulder. "Commander Bennet?"

He lifted his head to see the doctor standing next to his chair. "Dr. Hixsom. Is everything okay?" He'd been sleeping deeply and it was harder than normal to clear his mind. "How's Zaya?"

"Last I checked, her fever was down and she seemed to be responding to the antibiotics." He shifted from foot to foot, as if he was uneasy. Before he heard whatever the doctor was going to say, Julian stood, so he could face whatever it was head on.

The doctor stilled and let out a breath before he spoke. "The cuts and contusions on her left foot will take some time to heal properly. There's some nerve damage, and the chances of her ever being able to walk on it without limping are slim."

Julian let that information settle in his gut, adding it to the ball of rage toward Nazer that had formed there over the last few months, black and dense, waiting to be released. "What else?"

"She was caned, so she has some scarring and damage to her hands and back." He glanced over at Julian. "She's also severely dehydrated and underweight. In her weakened state, combined with the fever and infection, she might not have lasted much longer."

Even though they were in semi-darkness, he could see the doctor's jaw clench. He was reciting her injuries in a clinical tone, but he wasn't completely unruffled after treating her.

"Let me ask you this, Dr. Hixson," Julian started, before a familiar voice spoke from behind him.

"Are you interrogating my doctor?" Zaya tsked, sounding annoyed and out of breath. "Not very well done of you."

How had she come from the opposite direction without anyone seeing her leave her room?

"How did you . . ." He looked back at the door, then to her. "I thought you were resting."

"Couldn't sleep, so I thought I'd try to catch the next bus to Bagram. Just my luck there are no vehicles headed where I want to go." She shrugged her shoulders. "Story of my life these days."

"Who would want to go to Bagram, when you could be at a nearly deserted base with me?" Julian raised his eyebrows and gave her a small smile. She was making a joke. That was a good sign, wasn't it? "I thought you were giving me twenty-four hours to convince you to let me help."

"*You* said I was giving you twenty-four hours. I don't recall agreeing to that." She put her hand out and steadied herself on the wall. "And if accepting your help means that I give up my privacy so my doctor can give you detailed reports, I think I'll have to say no."

The doctor had the grace to look chagrined. "I apologize. Under normal circumstances . . ." He glanced at Julian. "Commander Bennet is very concerned for your well-being."

"I'm sure." She flipped on the hall light, and they all blinked in the brightness of it.

"You need to rest and get your strength back," Julian said. "And in order to make sure you have the best care, I need to know what your injuries are, so we can focus on getting you well."

"I don't need a mother, Julian. Or another jailer." She folded her arms across her chest, but leaned heavily against the wall behind her. "I think it best if I head to Bagram and work my way home from there. It will be easier. For both of us."

Julian's breath rushed out of him at the thought of her leaving so soon after he'd gotten her back, and the real chance he might lose her for good. "I won't ask the doctor another thing about your condition. I promise. Just let me take you back to England. I have a pilot that can fly you out of here tomorrow."

She stood in front of him, her eyes wide and troubled, as if she were contemplating his words. The urge to take her away, to hold her until she could laugh and smile with him again, was overpowering.

"I don't think I can be on the same plane as you." She bit her lip, her eyes not leaving his, as if trying to see something in his face.

His guts twisted at the words he knew he deserved. She blamed him so much for her suffering that she couldn't even be in the same vicinity as him. He needed her to see his regret and sorrow. It took all his energy to hold himself still, when he wanted to fall to his knees and beg her forgiveness. If there was any way he could go back in time and stay with her that day, he would. But all that wishing got him nowhere. All he could do now was try to help her in any way she would let him. "Z, please . . ."

She didn't let him finish, interrupting him with rushed words, coming out in one breath. "I need to leave everything and everyone connected to Nazer al-Raimi behind in Afghanistan."

Including me. She didn't have to say the words, they were written all over her face. The ache in his heart magnified. He stepped closer, wishing he dared touch her arm, but kept his eyes on her face. "I don't want to leave you alone until you're safe and healed."

"What if I don't want your company?" She stepped back, as if she wanted more physical distance between them to prove her words. But her eyes were vulnerable, revealing the deep hurt she had inside.

"If that's what you really want, Z," he said softly. She held his gaze for a second, then ducked her head and refused to answer. A tiny bit of hope rose in his chest. Maybe she hadn't written him off completely. Not that it mattered at this point. If there was any reason to think she'd let him comfort her, be with her, he wasn't going to leave. He couldn't.

The doctor cleared his throat uncomfortably. "Well, maybe I'll go and let you two work this out between yourselves." He turned to Zaya. "But I recommend going back to bed. Your body needs to rest and recover."

"I'll see she gets her proper rest," Julian said. He could at least do that much. But Zaya drew her brows down and frowned at his words, and he knew immediately he'd said the wrong thing.

"Is that an order, Julian?" The hand that was using the wall for support slid to her side and clenched into a fist. "Because I'm done taking orders. From anyone."

He held up both of his hands in surrender. "It's only a reassurance that someone is going to look out for you, okay? At least let me help you back to your room?" She looked so frail and probably felt worse.

She shook her head, a determined look on her face that made Julian want to groan aloud. When she dug in her heels, no one would change her mind. "I'll manage." She shuffle-limped toward the door. The doctor's diagnosis rang through Julian's head. Would her limp always be so pronounced? Were there physical therapy options that could help?

She opened the door and nearly stumbled, but caught herself. He inched closer, just in case she fell. He wanted to be there to catch her, to build trust between them again. She straightened, but the moment her left foot touched the floor, pain flashed in her eyes.

He pressed his lips together, but was unable to keep silent. "Can I carry you? If you've been running all over the hospital trying to hitch a ride, your feet could probably use a rest." He wondered how far she'd made it on her escape attempt before finally admitting defeat. He had to admire her grit, though. It was obvious, too, that she was still able to use her

Spec Ops training to remain as invisible as possible. No one had even noticed her missing.

"I don't need to be carried." She limped faster as if to prove it to him.

"You're still as stubborn as ever." He followed her into the room and stopped at the edge of her bed.

"I prefer single-minded," she said over her shoulder. "And you're one to talk." She gingerly climbed back under the blankets.

"If we had a contest over it, you'd win," he said confidently, glad to see another glimmer of the old Zaya.

"I'd win any contest against you," she muttered. "Everyone knows that."

He suppressed the urge to laugh.

"Julian's admitting he's not the best at something?" Colt asked, as the door whooshed shut behind him. "Glad I'm here to witness it then."

"Hey," Julian protested mildly.

Of all the team members, Colt was the most like him. He liked to make sure the people around him were taken care of physically and emotionally. But Colt had a fierce competitive streak not many people could match, and his slightly crooked nose from a past championship hockey game testified to the fact that he would go the distance no matter what.

He appeared relaxed as he strode over, skirting an empty gurney until he stopped next to Zaya's bed. He looked down at her, stroking his beard. It was getting long, but the facial hair helped him blend in with the locals, and Colt didn't seem to mind. "You two have a little friendly competition, then? Or is it not so friendly, eh?"

Julian shook his head at the loaded question and how Colt's Canadian accent slipped out every now and then. "Aren't you supposed to be monitoring our preparations for tomorrow's flight out of here? Is everything clear?" Julian asked.

Colt gave him a tolerant smile. "Yes, Commander. Perimeter is secure. We're on schedule, and all's quiet. I'm just reporting in."

Even with Colt's reassurance, a prickle of unease went down Julian's spine. Something was wrong. He couldn't explain how he knew, but he did.

Colt must have noticed his edginess and tried to reassure him. "It's fine, really. Brenna checked on the flight plans for tomorrow. I think everyone's ready to break camp and go home." He looked over at Zaya apologetically. "Unless you need another day or two of rest. We're happy to stick around as long as you need us."

Julian wasn't listening any longer. He went to the door and paused, peeking out into the hallway. Tension radiated through him, and he had the urge to run. His hand tightened on the doorknob as the floor rumbled beneath him. An explosion rocked the building.

"Get down," he shouted to Zaya as he sprinted back to her. Shielding her body with his own, he pulled her to the back of the room as another explosion went off. Footsteps sounded down the hallway, and Julian drew his gun. Someone was headed straight for them. He put his body between Zaya and whoever was coming through her door.

"Julian! Colt!" Jake barked out as he burst through the door. "You guys okay?"

Julian turned and looked back at Zaya. "I'm fine," she told him and stood back up. Yet, even with her best attempt to look okay, she still swayed and Julian put his arm around her, ostensibly to steady her, but also to reassure him that she wasn't hurt.

"What's going on out there?" Colt asked. "Everything was quiet when I left five minutes ago." He backed toward the opposite side of the room, picking his way through broken floor tiles.

"Nazer found us," Zaya said. Her voice was flat, the expression in her eyes lifeless. Any fire she'd regained was effectively snuffed out just saying his name.

"He's the likely suspect, but I think we should get out of here before we discuss it further." Jake said, as he joined Colt near the doorway. "That rocket brought down the entrance to the hospital. We're going to have to go out the back way."

Julian's arm tightened around Zaya's shoulders. "Can you make it?"

She shrugged him off and gave him an annoyed look. "Of course."

"Sorry." His hand hung at his side. He wanted to support her, but he was always doing the wrong thing.

50

She turned away from him and took a step toward Colt. "How did Nazer find us so quickly?" she asked him. "You'd think he'd need to go underground and regroup."

"The man's more slippery than a Canadian highway in December and just as treacherous. Who knows why he does what he does." Colt looked behind him. "Jake, we need to clear the way to get to the airfield, and we've got to go now. I'm going to alert everyone else to get to the hangars and evacuate to the planes."

They stepped into the hallway and Colt pushed forward, already talking into his radio while the rest of them followed, tense and on high alert. Both Jake and Julian kept their guns drawn and battle-ready. The scene in front of them was chaos. Gunfire was coming from outside and men were shouting. They were under attack, and there was no doubt what they'd come for. Nazer would like nothing better than to kill every member of Griffin Force– Julian and Zaya most of all. But that wasn't going to happen. Keeping Zaya close to his side, he did his best to skirt the worst of the combat zones and find a back exit.

They slipped down the halls, but the farther they went the more Zaya slowed down. It was obvious she was holding her breath every time she put weight on her left foot, trying to cope with the pain. Finally, Julian couldn't take it anymore. "Z, let me carry you. Please."

She bit her lip and nodded. The moment he had her permission, he scooped her into his arms. She practically melted against him with a sigh, a testament to how much of a toll this ordeal had taken on her physically and emotionally.

"I've got you," he murmured into her hair.

Jake looked back at them. "The exit's straight ahead."

Julian acknowledged he'd heard, and they carefully opened the door. The acrid smell of smoke met his nostrils, and he grimaced. This was definitely not how he'd imagined her rescue going. A quick stop to get her well enough to travel and then take her home. That had been his plan. Not fighting Nazer in the middle of an empty British airbase.

They stepped out into the open, but before they could go any farther, Julian heard a faint whistle.

"Run for the wall!" he shouted and he took off toward the airfield, pressing Zaya into his chest as he went. She clung to him, and he prayed he could get her clear. Her body and spirit had been through so much. He didn't want her hurt ever again.

The explosion sounded behind them, so close Julian's ears started ringing. He sprang forward and was barely able to roll himself and Zaya behind the wall that surrounded the hospital, while trying to shield her from any fallout. Smoke burned his throat, but all he could see was Zaya on the ground, blood trickling from her scalp.

"Z, talk to me. Are you all right?"

She didn't move, at first, and his heart sank. "No, no, no!" he heard himself shout. This couldn't be happening. Not now. He turned her toward him.

"Julian?" Her eyes were unfocused, but open.

The rush of relief nearly undid him. "I'm here," he said, pushing away his own feelings to focus on her. He visually checked her for any more injuries. Beyond the small amount of blood on her head and the bruises she had when she arrived, he didn't see anything new, but head injuries were tricky. He looked around for Jake. They needed to get everyone out, now.

He leaned close. "Z, we're going to have to make a run for the hangar and stay on the perimeter. I don't want those rockets lighting up our aircraft before we can get in the air."

She looked up at him, dirty and bloodied, her eyes miserable and afraid. "I can't make it, Julian. My foot is shredded." She lifted a shoulder. "I should be heroic and say you should just leave me here, but I can't go back to that prison."

He let his thumb caress her cheek for just a moment. "I'm not leaving you." He got to his feet and lifted her with him.

She put her arms around him, and if the world hadn't been burning down around them, he might have enjoyed that sensation more, especially when she buried her face in his neck.

"Thank you," she said, just loudly enough for him to hear.

With those two words echoing in his ears, the sliver of hope he'd had from earlier widened considerably. He held her slight body close to his heart and started running.

CHAPTER FIVE

Zaya tried desperately to shut out the pandemonium and shouting behind her. Instead, she turned her head into the spot between Julian's neck and shoulder and inhaled. He still wore his spicy cologne from Harrod's. The smell washed her in happy memories, but even good memories wouldn't do her any good if she were re-captured. Her hold on him tightened as the gunfire sounded closer.

"Almost there," Julian said, as he readjusted her weight.

She cursed her wounded feet, wishing she were running alongside him. From what she'd overheard the doctor saying, though, that would never happen again. At that thought, she tucked the ache in her heart away to examine later.

Another explosion sounded, but not as close as before. Nazer was here. She knew it. Pressing her ear closer to Julian's chest, she tried to block the panic that was threatening to overtake her sensibilities. Her heart was already beating so hard she couldn't breathe.

The Capture

Just hang on to Julian. He was her anchor in the storm. She used all of her concentration to focus on her breathing and the feel of Julian's arms securely holding her.

She didn't open her eyes again until they boarded the plane and Julian set her down onto an extra-wide seat. It was quieter here, and her senses weren't quite so overloaded.

"This isn't military," she commented, glad her voice sounded steady as she looked around. In fact, it wasn't a commercial plane, either. The cabin was larger, and the seats were clustered in groups of four. "Is this a private plane?"

"I use it for missions, but yes." Julian was searching in the overhead compartment and finally pulled out a towel and blanket. He handed her the towel. "Put this on your head to stop the bleeding."

"Thanks." She hadn't noticed how much blood there was until she looked at his t-shirt where her head had been.

He handed her the blanket next. "As soon as we're in the air, I'll have Elliott look at that cut on your head."

Zaya looked up at him, her mind blurring the present with the past. The guard in her prison cell handing her a ratty blanket, and Julian's hand suddenly morphed into the guard's hairy hand. She gasped, pushing down an impulse to hit him, hurt him. Trying to focus on the present, she centered her mind on the thick softness of the blanket she'd accepted from Julian.

I'm safe now, she told herself, tucking the blanket around her.

"Hey, what's wrong?" Julian asked, his voice full of concern. Her eyes met his, and for just a second it was as if he knew her thoughts, how weak she'd been while she was imprisoned. He stood there, strong and tall, everything she wasn't anymore, and anger roiled inside her. At the same time, though, a tiny traitorous part of her wanted him to hold her. She wanted to lean on him, to let him comfort her, but she tamped that feeling down. Her emotions were too volatile. A minute ago she'd wanted to hurt him for offering her a blanket. She had a lot to sort out before she let anyone close, especially him.

Julian was staring at her, and she squirmed under his gaze. "I'm fine," she said, hoping to sound convincing.

He looked back toward the pilot. "I need to make sure the team made it on board and the forces I hired for ground support can hold them off until we're in the air."

"You don't need to babysit me." Her voice sounded resentful even to her own ears, and she brushed her hands over the blanket. *Stay calm.* "I'm not going anywhere."

He cocked his head and with one last concerned look for her, went to check on the team. The airplane's engines roared to life, and she looked out the window, grateful to be getting underway. There hadn't been any more explosions, but she could still hear faint gunfire. The plane started to move, but she didn't feel safe yet, and wouldn't until they were out of Afghanistan.

The plane rumbled over the uneven ground and Julian headed down the aisle toward her. "Did the team make it in?" she asked Julian when he rejoined her.

"Everyone is accounted for. Elliott's on the other plane with the injured." He sat in the seat across from Zaya, his knees almost touching hers. "I wanted him to come check the cut on your head."

"It's nothing. He can see it when we land." She lowered the towel and there wasn't an alarming amount of blood on it. All she really wanted was to feel the plane lift off and take her far away from Nazer.

As if he could read her thoughts, Julian leaned closer. "Next stop, jolly old England. There isn't anywhere better for rest and recuperation."

Back to her life. What was left of it, anyway. "Can I stay in the safehouse in West London? Just until I get on my feet." The little flat was small and nondescript, but at this point, she didn't care where she stayed, as long as she was in England and not Afghanistan.

"Actually, I bought a small estate in Surrey. I was thinking you could recuperate there. It's private, and you'll be safe." He didn't meet her eyes as he spoke. There was something he wasn't telling her.

"An estate?" Zaya raised an eyebrow. "Finally living up to your family connections, are you?" One of Julian's ancestors had been a duke or something, but he'd always been reluctant to talk about it.

"It ended up being a business transaction, but the place is out of the way and perfect for the rest and recovery you need right now," he said. He looked at her, worry in his eyes. Warmth and caring shadowed their depths, but he was speaking with care, as if he didn't want to say something wrong. Was he trying to gain some emotional distance? Maybe he'd finally realized that they couldn't ever go back to where they were before she'd been abducted. The thought depressed her a little.

Unresolved feelings still hung between them, though. The air crackled with all the words that were unsaid. She raised her chin. It was true she couldn't give him the closeness he wanted, but she could try to reassure him of her well-being. That way, when they did part, maybe it wouldn't be difficult for him. "Don't worry. I'm going to be fine," she said softly, hoping to chase some of his worries away.

He rolled his shoulders, as if he was getting ready to say something important. "I know you will, Z, but I just can't . . . I want to . . ." He looked away. "Never mind. I'm going to check with Colt to find out what happened back there." He bolted out of his seat and strode away.

Zaya thought briefly about calling him back. What was Julian about to say? He couldn't what? But her tongue couldn't form the words. Both of them were obviously struggling to reconcile what had been between them with what was in front of them now, and they'd come to a shaky truce at best. But every time she was near him, her reactions were intense and powerful. At some point, they'd have to get things worked out or she'd never be able to move on.

Not that moving on was an option at the moment. Zaya closed her eyes. Nazer wasn't out of their lives. He'd gotten close again. Too close. The attack at the base had to have been orchestrated by him. It seemed like there wasn't anywhere Julian or Zaya could hide that he wouldn't find them, and that made her misgivings about Julian's plans to take her to his safe house ratchet up a little higher. He'd easily found Julian at the base. What if Nazer found them in England? At least there they had some allies and protections they didn't have in Afghanistan.

Fear rose in her again, and she looked around the cabin as if Nazer would suddenly pop up from behind her and finish what he'd started in that filthy cell. Her heart rate picked up, and her chest felt like it was being squeezed. Zaya clenched her fists.

Don't think about it. She rubbed her temples to calm herself, then huddled under the blanket as if she could hide from her own thoughts.

Keeping her eyes open and trying to blank her mind from her fears of re-capture, she focused on Julian and Colt. Whatever Colt was saying made Julian scowl enough to make it obvious he didn't like what he was hearing. Wishing she were closer, she strained to hear even a snatch of the conversation.

"Hi, Z," a female voice came from her left. She startled, a little yelp escaping, and put her hand to her chest. Within seconds, Julian was by her side.

"I'm sorry, I didn't mean to sneak up on you like that." Brenna Wilson slowly sat down, her hands out in a conciliatory manner.

"It's okay. I'm just feeling a little jumpy." Zaya forced herself to relax. "Brenna, right?" The other woman had been a recruit from Canada, if Zaya remembered correctly. She looked up at Julian standing over her like a mother hen and frowned. "I'm okay. You don't need to hover."

He didn't answer, but he did sit down. "We're far enough away from the gunfight we can take off." His words were abrupt, but Zaya felt relief. They were going to get out of here.

Buckling in, he turned to Brenna. "You got here just in time for the fun."

"Wouldn't miss it." She glanced over at Zaya. "What happened?"

"We're still working out the details." His answer was smooth, but Zaya could tell he didn't want to discuss it in front of her. The fire of annoyance started in her belly, and she folded her arms.

"You know, I've been wondering that myself." Zaya raised an eyebrow at Julian. "Was it Nazer or is someone else anxious to kill us?"

He drummed his fingers on the armrest and tilted his head, trying to read her tone. "Details are still sketchy. Augie has a few leads, but we're still gathering intelligence. I don't want to jump to any conclusions."

Of course he was right. The fire went out of Zaya. Was she paranoid on top of everything else? "That makes sense," she mumbled, her voice small. Long ago, she'd been the one admonishing Julian not to jump to conclusions on a case. The shoe was definitely on the other foot now.

The Capture

The engines roared, and the plane picked up speed. Zaya resisted the urge to grab the armrests. For some reason that seemed like a show of weakness, and she didn't want to project that in front of Julian. But actually being able to feel strong and capable was like a shadow she couldn't grasp.

"No matter who it was, I don't want you to worry. Just concentrate on getting well. I'll take care of the rest." Julian's voice was a little too bright. He didn't want her to worry, but he definitely was.

"Nazer slithers in and out of anywhere, you know that," Zaya said grimly. The terrorist was living up to his reputation and sending a message: they couldn't hide from him. Fear was his weapon, and he used it well.

"We don't know it was him," Julian said, finally turning to look at her. "You're right, there aren't a lot of other groups that would attempt that kind of attack, but it could be the Taliban or an al-Qaeda offshoot with a grudge against us. It's good to be thorough before we think of retaliation."

"We both know this was a message from Nazer." There wasn't any doubt in her mind. She turned back to the window.

What am I going to do?

"Whatever you're thinking, stop," Julian ordered. "We need more information before drawing any conclusions. And we're going to face whatever comes together."

There were so many things she wanted to point out to him. She'd already been facing Nazer on her own for six months. Why did he think it was better to stay together now where they would be a bigger and easier target? But she stayed quiet. He was right. They needed more information before they could figure out the next step.

"To tell you the truth, I have a lot of decisions to make about what comes next for me, and I would appreciate you keeping me in the loop about Nazer. He's stolen so much . . ." She loathed having to talk about that man when all she wanted to do was erase him from her life. "I need to know what I'm facing, so I can make informed decisions, that's all."

He leaned forward at that. "Nazer has always been *our* problem. We're a team, Z. Remember?"

His arms were folded, and he had that stubborn look on his face, but she could be just as stubborn. Before she could argue her case, though, Brenna shifted forward and touched her arm.

"Z, I brought you some clothes. Would you like to wash up and change?"

Zaya narrowed her eyes and nodded, deciding to let it go with Julian for now. She looked down at her dirty and bloody clothing she'd barely put on a few hours ago. "Thanks. Although I'll miss these scrubs. Green is my favorite color and they are pretty comfy."

Brenna gave her a half-smile. "I know, right? Don't you wish we could wear them all the time and not have people ask us for medical advice?"

Zaya laughed and for just a second felt like her old self— until Julian cut in. "There's a bathroom just beyond those curtains. You might have a concussion, and with your foot . . ." He looked down at it, then back at her. "Maybe I should carry you? Just to be safe."

He said it as if it were normal, something he was going to do for the rest of his life—and there was no way she'd ever let that happen. "I've got this, thanks." She stood and gritted her teeth against the pain in her feet. Brenna stood with her, then bent down to grab a bag from the floor.

"We'll be right back," Brenna said over her shoulder to Julian. They made their way to the bathroom. It was slow-going, but Brenna kept pace with her. Zaya could feel Julian's eyes on her, but she didn't turn around to look.

When they made it to the bathroom, Brenna handed her the bag. "I'm here if you ever need to talk."

Zaya gave Brenna a smile. "Thanks, I appreciate that." She gingerly reached out to pat Brenna's arm before heading inside the bathroom and shutting the door. It was bigger than a commercial airline bathroom, and she was grateful she wouldn't have to do some sort of pseudo-yoga poses to get changed.

She unzipped the bag and took out a plain blue T-shirt and a pair of jeans, along with some socks and underwear. She fingered the T-shirt material, trying to memorize the feel of it against her skin. It wasn't anything special—the same type of cotton she'd put on without a second thought almost her entire life. But in this moment, it was strange. New. Cool to the touch. Tears pricked the back of her throat, and then they were spilling over her cheeks. Zaya swiped at them, anger filling her and driving the sadness away. She wasn't going to cry over clothing. She didn't want to cry ever again.

Looking at herself in the small mirror above the sink, she barely recognized the woman reflected. Brown eyes that looked too large for her face stared back. Fire and determination had been replaced by fear and frustration. Bruises and scrapes covered her, reminding her of where she'd been.

The woman in the mirror was a different person. Yet, instead of alternating between feeling angry and mourning for what she'd lost, Zaya needed to find a way to embrace what she'd become. There had to be a hidden well of strength she could still draw on.

In all her years of working her way up the British military intelligence ranks, and then winning a place in Griffin Force, she hadn't doubted she could do it. That was the attitude she needed. And while the woman staring back at her didn't look or feel strong, she *was* a survivor. And Zaya needed to start acting like one.

After removing her dirty hospital scrubs, she washed the grime from her body and dressed, leaving the old clothes behind in a garbage can. This was her new beginning, and she was going to do everything she could to forge a new future for herself.

CHAPTER SIX

Julian couldn't sit still. He tried to keep himself busy, but his thoughts and energy were centered on Zaya and her needs. After she'd returned from the bathroom, he watched her smile at Brenna. It made his heart squeeze. For a second, she looked much more like the woman she'd been, casual and happy. But he knew that after her experiences in captivity, she was neither of those things, and that's what haunted him.

He could still feel the shape of her in his arms from when he'd carried her to the plane, and he ached to hold her again. He had to be patient, though, and earn her trust, her forgiveness. He'd seen little glimpses of possibility and that was enough to keep him hoping.

It had taken every ounce of restraint he had to patch up the small gash in her hairline and not kiss it better, or keep her in his arms afterward, until she felt better. She'd been so tense he'd pushed all that aside and been as clinical as possible. Afterward, they'd raided the galley for a midflight snack and Zaya had taken several packages of crackers and set them on the seat next to her. Her eyes occasionally darted to the food, as if to make sure it was still there, an after-effect of being starved. Another little bullet of rage added to the ball simmering inside him at what she'd gone through. He was going to make this right.

Julian took out his laptop and tried to do some work so it wouldn't seem as if he was "hovering," as she'd accused him of doing. She was quiet, contemplative, and not long after she rested her head against the window, he realized she'd fallen asleep.

She was so still, he started to watch the blanket for its repeated rise and fall as she breathed. He kept watch over her sleeping form most of the flight, grateful she was finally getting some rest.

Just before they landed in England, Colt came and sat next to him. He glanced over at Zaya before turning to Julian. "She's going to be okay," he said softly. "She's strong. She survived."

"I know." He shifted in his seat, not wanting to talk about her with anyone. "Is everything ready for landing?"

"Yes. We have four cars meeting us at the airport." Colt's eyes were full of sympathy, but he allowed the subject change. "I think we're all looking forward to some downtime. Do you think Zaya will really want all of us at the house?"

Julian definitely wanted them all there to protect Zaya. "We need to do an after action review and discuss where to go from here. It's just easier to have us all in one location for that."

Zaya pulled in a breath and opened her eyes, blinking slowly as she focused on him. He lowered his voice slightly. "The house is set on forty acres, so we'll have plenty of room for training, too."

Colt groaned. "So much for R and R."

Zaya stretched, the blanket falling to her waist. "Julian always was a little tyrannical." She pulled it back up, as if it were a shield. "Are we close?"

"Hey, I prefer to think of myself as a *benevolent* tyrant, at least. And we should be landing momentarily." Julian cocked his head. "How are you feeling?"

"Fine," she said automatically.

He didn't believe her. Anyone could see that the color in her cheeks was high. Her fever was probably back. He didn't contradict her though. The best thing he could do for her was to get her to the house where she could get the rest and care she needed.

The plane began its descent, and they all buckled in. Zaya white-knuckled it until they touched down. Julian wanted to do something to help her, but he gave her space. *Patience*, he reminded himself.

When they were finally on the ground, Julian disembarked to make sure their transition to the cars went smoothly. Elliott approached him on the tarmac. Everything about him was average– average brown hair, average height– but that worked well for someone on an elite task force when he needed to blend in. He had a stammer, which came out when he was under stress, but his medical skills were second to none in the field. He'd saved each member of the team at one time or another. It calmed Julian to have him nearby for Zaya.

Today, Elliott's stammer was evident and he took a moment before he spoke. "J-J-Julian, I need to go with a p-patient to Frimley Park hospital." Elliott rummaged through his medical bag and put some supplies in Julian's hand. "Here's something for Zaya's fever and extra bandages. I should be able to meet you at the house by tomorrow morning."

Julian's stomach tightened. He could see Elliott was really worried, and that added another layer of guilt that Julian hadn't followed up about anyone else's injuries. "What's wrong?"

"Charlie's l-leg was broken in the explosion. I set it as best I could, b-but it might need surgery."

"Charlie?" Julian furrowed his brow. He couldn't remember a Charlie on the team, and Griffin Force wasn't so large that he couldn't recall names.

A flush appeared on Elliott's neck. "Charlotte Flynn. She's a n-nurse."

Recognition dawned. He remembered her, a competent nurse who always had a calm air around her.

Julian put his hand on Elliott's shoulder. "Go with Charlie, but keep me informed on her status. Any other injuries I need to know about?"

"Nothing serious, mostly m-minor burns, cuts, and contusions." His attention was riveted to the plane, where people were starting to file out.

"Do you need me to call an ambulance?"

"I think I can d-drive." He turned back to Julian. "Do you m-mind if I take one of the cars?"

"Not at all." He stepped back. "Report in when you have more information."

"Will d-do." He jogged back toward the other plane, and Julian gave the all clear. He wanted to get Zaya to the house as soon as possible.

Once they were all bundled into a car, he let himself relax. She sat next to him, her warm body pressed close as they fit Colt in on her other side.

"I'm so cold," she said, her teeth chattering as she burrowed into the warmth of his side.

"Your fever's back," he said, touching her forehead. "Elliott left some medicine for you. We're going to get you fixed up as soon as we get to the house." He stretched out an arm and pulled her close.

She looked up at him, her cheeks flushed. "I'm always so cold. I thought I'd freeze to death in that cell."

He stroked her hair, wishing her eyes weren't so haunted. "Let me warm you up."

"You're the only warm place in the world," she mumbled.

The Capture

Julian's rib cage squeezed. His head knew it was the fever talking, but his heart still skipped a beat to hear her say the words.

She settled her head on his shoulder, and he decided to just enjoy the moment. The car ride wasn't long, and when they made it up the long driveway, he got out and reached back to carry her. The moment he touched her, worry over her fever jumped to fear. She was burning up. He needed to get her inside.

He tucked her body close and shifted her in his arms so he could take the key out of his pocket. Opening the door, he strode through the formal living room and headed for the stairs. Hopefully his people had had enough time to finish all his orders and the blue bedroom was ready for her. Zaya tipped her head back to look at him, the fever making her eyes look glazed.

"Either you've been working out or I've lost some weight." She patted his bicep.

"Maybe a little bit of both." Striding down the hall, Julian was grateful when he finally walked through the bedroom door; the room was clean and welcoming. He laid her on the bed, the smell of freshly laundered sheets hitting his nose. "Elliott left some ibuprofen and an antibiotic for you." He turned to the nightstand and grabbed a bottle of water. After he handed it to her, he took the pills from the bag of supplies Elliott had given him. "Take these."

"My foot hurts. Can't fly a plane," she murmured, but she took the pills and laid down, her eyes closed. The fever must be high. She sounded delirious and his uneasiness ratcheted up.

"We're going to take care of that." He took her hand, so small in his. Even her fingers were hot from fever.

"Saif wants to know how many people are on Griffin Force. Where you like to keep your money. How you recruit. Your cat's name." She frowned. "No, not the cat. I'll never tell him Milo's name."

Julian drew his eyebrows together. Nazer wanted to know about his cat? Or was that the fever talking?

She squeezed his hand and pulled away. He felt the loss immediately and wanted to take it again, but folded his hands in his lap instead. She leaned forward as if she were going to tell him a secret and whispered, "I won't tell them. Julian will come for me, and I'll tell him how I protected Milo."

"You did great," he assured her. He didn't need a thermometer to tell him that her fever must be dangerously high. Combined with her infection and malnutrition, it was to be expected, but it didn't make him any less worried. He wished Elliott were here. For the moment, she was stuck with him.

He tentatively reached out to brush back a piece of hair from her face. She didn't flinch away, which he took as a good sign. "You survived that cell, and Milo is safe and sound. You don't have to worry about anything." His parents had looked after the old cat while he'd searched for Zaya, and now that he'd found her, he wasn't going to leave.

Julian picked up the bottled water again. She needed to get some liquid in her and avoid dehydration. "Z, can you take a drink for me?" He put his arm around her shoulders and lifted her head.

She took a dainty sip, then coughed. "I'm just so cold."

"Let me get you a blanket." He started to ease her back, but she gripped the front of his shirt.

"No. Please. Don't leave me again."

She closed her eyes and sagged against him, as if saying the words had cost every bit of energy she had. Julian's heart cracked down the middle. She looked so vulnerable in his arms. He lightly kissed her forehead. "I won't leave you. I'm right here." He maneuvered the sheet out from under her, careful not to jostle her too much, and pulled it on top of her. He sat next to her on the bed, and she snuggled into his side.

"You're so warm," she whispered. "I would have done anything to be warm in that cell."

Had it really only been a day since they'd gotten her back? His arms involuntarily tightened around her, trying to give her all the warmth she needed. It took several minutes, but her shivering started to abate. Julian didn't want to move, though. Having her in his arms was more along the lines of how he'd imagined their reunion. Holding her. Comforting her. Loving her. No blame or guilt between them. He gently brushed his knuckles over her cheek as he listened to her breathing even out as she fell asleep. They'd always been stronger together. That's what he wanted her to remember.

A few minutes later, there was a soft knock on the door, and Julian reluctantly eased away from her and went to answer it.

"How are things?" Colt asked, a thread of concern in his voice.

"Hopefully the medicine kicks in sooner rather than later. I'm worried about how high her fever is." Julian shoved his hands in his pockets and glanced back at her. "I don't have a thermometer because I thought Elliott would be with us."

"She's got the medicine running through her system and she'll probably sleep for a while," Colt said. "Why don't you come downstairs? You haven't eaten a decent meal in days."

"I don't want her to wake up alone in a strange house," he explained. "Can you tell Jake to divvy out the bedrooms downstairs? It's Nate's turn to bunk with Augie, and Brenna and Mya can have the other two rooms on this floor. I made up shifts for patrolling the perimeter, but we need to make everyone aware of the schedule."

"You worried about Nazer finding us here?" Colt asked, pausing before he turned to go back downstairs.

"Never hurts to be careful where he's concerned." Julian looked over at Zaya again. "If he tried to attack us at Bastion Air Base, he's not as immobilized as we thought. We've got some loose ends. See if any leads Augie's following have panned out."

"Okay. I'll let you know what I find." Colt left, and the room fell quiet. Julian walked as silently as possible back to her. Sunlight was starting to peek through the curtains, laying a stripe of warmth on the wood floor. It felt strange to finally be in this house with Zaya, but there was also a rightness to it. He pulled up a chair and settled himself next to the bed, unable to keep his eyes off her sleeping form.

With her hair short it made her cheekbones stand out more, the gauntness a testimony that she hadn't eaten regularly. She was still beautiful to him, yet he had to push down all the emotions that surfaced whenever he thought about what she'd endured. He had to keep his focus away from that, but they'd both been irrevocably affected by her captivity. He was a little more optimistic than she was they might be able to work through all the collateral damage and find their way back to each other. Maybe they couldn't. But he had to try.

There was another soft knock at the door, and Julian rose to see who it was before they could wake Zaya. Brenna waited expectantly in the hall, and he joined her, closing the door behind him.

"How is she?" Brenna asked.

"Sleeping. Exhausted. Feverish." He leaned against the wall. "How are things going downstairs?"

"Mrs. Finch has arrived, and she's organizing the boys. Was she in the military?" Brenna's eyebrows rose. "She has a certain demeanor, and when she's giving orders, no one dares say no."

Mrs. Finch did have the bearing of a duke or a general, come to think of it. Like a female Wellington. "Not that I know of. She's a therapist at the Intensive Treatment Center for PTSD, though, so she works with a lot of military people, I imagine. I want her to try to help Zaya." And he hoped she'd take advantage of Mrs. Finch. If anyone could help Zaya heal, she could.

"Does Zaya know you have a therapist here?" Brenna asked, folding her arms. "She might not be ready for that."

"It can't hurt to at least introduce them," Julian said. "After Zaya's feeling better, of course."

"Well, when I left, Mrs. Finch was making a pot of tea and English biscuits. Very proper. Colt was hanging around the kitchen to get the first bite. A lot of people might feel better with her in the house."

"It's probably the first home cooking Colt's had in weeks. Unless you cooked him something, of course," Julian amended.

Brenna gave him the side-eye. "He's not starving. The man has a sugar addiction, though, and it sounds like Mrs. Finch's baking is going to aid and abet his cravings."

"Maybe she's trying to make a good impression. Tea and biscuits *are* an English staple, you know. Colt is just trying to fit in while we're here."

Brenna snorted. "Whatever. Do you want me to bring you up a tray or anything?"

"Thanks, that would be great. I don't want to leave her right now." He looked back at the bedroom door.

"I get it." Brenna started back down the hallway. "You know, you look pretty exhausted yourself. You should try to get some rest."

"Thanks." Julian ran a hand through his hair and went back into the bedroom. His body had been pushed to the limits today, and he was beyond exhausted. He paused at the door. Zaya wasn't still any longer. She was moving restlessly on the bed, the sheets clutched in her hands.

"No," she murmured. "No. Don't."

Julian was at her bedside in an instant and lay next to her, pulling her hair back to whisper in her ear. "It's okay now. I've got you. Just rest." What demons was she fighting in her sleep?

He put his arms around her and rocked her against his chest. She quieted, letting out a deep sigh before turning to rest her head against his bicep. He let a finger trail down her jawbone and pressed a kiss to her brow. Maybe he'd hold her a little longer and make sure she was calm, before he got in the chair next to the bed. But the moment he closed his eyes with Zaya in his arms, his body relaxed, and he fell asleep.

CHAPTER SEVEN

Zaya woke up, and her first conscious thought was that someone was holding her down, ready to inject her with drugs or strap her to that table again—*Saif!* She jammed her elbow into the man's gut and shot off the bed, nearly falling when her feet touched the floor and burning pain radiated up her leg. A tea tray was on the nightstand and she grabbed for a butterknife, causing the tray to crash to the floor. Frantically she scrambled for the makeshift weapon, as her captor moved toward her.

"Z, it's me, Julian. It's okay."

Dazed, his voice washed over her, penetrating her nightmare. She looked up at him, his familiar brown eyes full of concern. Sunshine filtered through the curtains. She remembered. They were in England. She was safe.

Footsteps pounded up the stairs, and Colt burst through the door with his gun drawn. "Julian!"

Julian held up his arm. "We're fine. Zaya knocked over the tray, that's all."

A flush crept up Zaya's face. She slowly put the knife on the edge of the nightstand. Her senses were on overload, and adrenaline was rushing through her. Taking a breath, she knelt and started picking up the food and dishes. "Sorry about that."

More people crowded into the doorway, but one imperious voice cut through them all. "Let me through, please."

A small woman, her gray hair pulled back in a bun, came through the crowd and crouched in front of her. She didn't seem concerned about the mess, but met Zaya's eyes. "Good morning. I'm Mrs. Finch." Then she proceeded to help pick up the dishes.

"Good morning," Zaya murmured. She glanced at Julian, but he was moving toward Colt, Jake, and Brenna at the door.

"I was hoping we'd be introduced today," Mrs. Finch said, when they were finished. "You weren't feeling very well yesterday."

Zaya tried to smooth down her hair. The fever. It was all starting to come back to her. "I'm better today."

Mrs. Finch patted her arm. "That's good. I'm going to have Commander Bennet bring you some breakfast, but before he does that, why don't you clean yourself up a bit? You'll feel better."

"Yes, ma'am," was all Zaya could think of to say.

Julian had shooed the rest of the team out of the room, and then he helped her to a chair. "Are you sure you're okay?"

"Just had a nightmare," she told him, ducking her head. She felt sweaty and gross, and he looked as if he'd rolled out of bed fresh and ready for the day.

"I get those sometimes, too," he said softly.

Her eyes flew to his. He hadn't had nightmares before— at least none she knew of. Were they another consequence of her abduction?

His hand slid up her arm, for comfort and reassurance, but she shivered in response. His fingers on her skin made her heart skip a beat, and his gaze held her mesmerized. The expression on his face was full of worry, and he brought his hand to her forehead, but his touch made her want more than his concern. For a moment, she imagined closing her eyes and letting go, drawing him closer, kissing him until she could forget the last few months. Her breathing quickened at the thought, and his eyes darkened as he watched her. The air around them suddenly charged with awareness.

"Seems like the fever's gone." Was his voice huskier than it had been, or was that her imagination?

Mrs. Finch noisily arranged the dishes on the tray. The effect was like pouring cold water on Zaya. How could she even think of pulling Julian in when she was such a mess? She'd nearly attacked him ten minutes ago.

"I feel much better today." She sucked in a breath and straightened to put some distance between them. This close, it was hard to remember why she was holding him at arms' length.

Julian dropped his hand, watching her carefully, but giving her the space she needed.

"Mrs. Finch mentioned you were going to bring up some breakfast." Her voice sounded raspier than she would have liked and she swallowed.

"I have some lovely porridge," Mrs. Finch said as she picked up the ruined tray of food and started to leave. "I'll go make sure it's ready for you." She gave Julian a glance as she walked away and left the door open, a silent invitation for Julian to follow.

He didn't seem to notice Mrs. Finch's hint since his focus was on Zaya, as if waiting for her to say something.

"I really am sorry about this morning," she murmured.

He tried to smooth his hair, but running a hand through it only succeeded in making him look more appealing, like those models on a GQ cover—deliberately rumpled, but still devastatingly gorgeous. "I'm sure it was a shock to wake up next to me, but, just so we're clear, I didn't take advantage of the fact you had a high fever and weren't yourself. You were thrashing about in your sleep, so I just held you for a moment until you quieted. I fully intended to sleep in the chair."

"It's fine." She'd been thrashing about? Had she said anything during her nightmare? She tried to ask, but the words stuck in her throat. The fragments of her dreams she could remember were ones she wanted to forget. Analyzing them with Julian wouldn't help, so she stayed quiet. Instead, she said, "Not to complain, but must my first real meal back in England be porridge?"

He smiled, and her heart stuttered at the sight of it. "Your hearty English constitution needs some building back up, and porridge is the cure-all, you know that." He stood up, so she had to crane her neck to look at him from her seated position. "I think the worry is that your stomach isn't used to more solid foods."

He winced slightly, as if he was reluctant to bring up the fact she hadn't eaten a decent meal in months. It made her want to tell him it was okay, but she couldn't. It wasn't okay. It would never be okay.

"But if you like, I might be convinced to bring you a scone with your porridge. That should be all right, don't you think?" He smiled.

"Scones are good," she said slowly. "But what's the possibility of getting a custard tart? I've been thinking of those for months." Her mouth watered at the thought of her favorite treat. "I don't want you to go to any trouble, though."

"Isn't it a little early for dessert?" He crouched down to her eye-level again, as if he couldn't quite bring himself to leave her yet, his eyebrows raised at her request. She shook her head, and he gave her a mock sigh and a chuckle. "If you must know, I had the house stocked with them." He was pleased with himself, and she couldn't help but smile back. He'd remembered her near-obsession with those tarts. "I'll go grab some for you." Standing, he gave her one more look, as if he were afraid she'd disappear if he left her alone, and then he shut the door behind him.

Zaya's smile dissipated, and she let out a breath. Being near him, but unable to trust herself not to hurt him, was exquisite new torture. She needed to get out of here. What if she'd turned the scalpel or even the butterknife on Julian? Yet, even if things were different and she could trust herself, what could she offer him now? From what the doctor said, she was a cripple, unable to walk normally. If nothing else, she should spare him being shackled to her for the long recovery and physical therapy she would need. But every look, every touch, reminded her of what they'd once shared. He was too close, yet where else could she go?

Gingerly stepping on her feet, she headed to the bathroom and locked the door, marveling at everything inside. Flushing toilets. A shower. Just glancing around the room caused her heart to flood with gratitude. She maneuvered to the sink, where a stack of clothes and towels waited on the counter. It was exactly what she'd been looking for. Stripping off her clothing and taking the bandages from her feet, she quickly turned the shower on as hot as she could stand it and stepped in. The heat was like heaven, and the pounding water cleansed her skin. Her feet stung, but she ignored them as best she could, reveling in the other sensations. After reaching for the soap, Zaya scrubbed her skin until it was red, anxious to feel clean again. She stood there, remembering her filthy cell, the darkness, the despair. She let herself cry. The shower spray turned cold, pulling her back to the present, and yet, the tears continued to run down her face. She was home. She was safe. Thirty-six hours ago, she'd been barely more than a caged animal, but it was behind her now.

Stepping out, she wiped the evidence of tears from her face, feeling cleansed, stronger, and more her old self. Even her feet felt better. The antibiotic Elliott had given her must be working. With renewed energy, she quickly dried and dressed. Hushed voices coming from the bedroom made her pause. It was too much of a temptation. She crept over to listen.

"Nazer put a hit out on Zaya. Adding to the one he already had on you."

The voice was Colt's, Zaya decided, having focused on identifying the speaker while pushing down the emotions that rose up at his words. Concentrating on hearing more, she maneuvered closer to the door and silently cracked it open. She was right. Colt and Julian stood in the middle of the room.

"How does Nazer have any money left to do anything besides buy himself a coffee?" Julian ran his hands through his hair again. "We dismantled every training ground, every safe house, and froze all his assets from his shell companies. There's no way he can have anything left."

"Unless he has a backer. He must also have a mole that's close to us. What other explanation could there be for how he's stayed one step ahead of us?" Colt folded his arms, nearly eye to eye with Julian.

"But who could it be?" Julian clenched his fists. "We're so careful. We've combed over every financial transaction, questioned everyone associated with Nazer in any way."

Colt pressed his lips together in thought. "I don't think it's an informant. It has to be someone in the intelligence community. Well-connected. Look at how quickly Nazer found us at Camp Bastion."

Julian groaned in frustration. "I know. There were only a handful of people who knew about that stopover. I'll have to take another look at all of them."

Colt shifted toward the fireplace, like he wanted to pace, but decided against it. "Maybe England isn't the best place for Zaya to be until we know who this backer is."

"She needed to come home, and I still think hiding in plain sight is the best defense for now." Julian sounded confident, but his words were tinged with concern. He wasn't sure about how safe she was in England. Even the thought of Nazer finding them made a frisson of panic skitter through her bones.

"At least we know he's looking, so we can prepare." Colt started to move toward the door. "I'll let the team know. Are you going to tell Zaya?"

"I don't want to worry her. She needs to concentrate on healing." But the words died on his lips when she opened the bathroom door wider to reveal herself.

"You don't have to baby me, Julian." Her words were harsher than she'd anticipated, but she needed him to hear her. "If I'm in danger, I deserve to know."

"You're not," he said, taking a step toward her. "I've got everything covered."

"I'll check in with you later." Colt looked between the two of them and quietly left without any acknowledgment.

Zaya limped to the chair in the corner of the room, cursing the wounds on her feet. She wanted to appear strong and capable, not hobbling and weak. "I need to be prepared for what's ahead, especially with the possibility Nazer's coming for me. To do that, though, I need information. Talk to me."

"I'll tell you everything you want to know, after you've eaten breakfast." Julian nodded to the tray on the small table by the window. "I even brought you a scone and a tart, as promised."

Zaya's stomach grumbled. "Why don't you tell me everything while I'm eating?" she countered.

He let out a breath. "How did I know you were going to say that?" He sat in the chair opposite her, and she scooted in. Even though the food in front of her was porridge, Zaya was happy to see it.

"So, why don't we start from the beginning. When I was . . . when I *left* . . ." She paused, not wanting to say *captured*. "Bahnini was killed in Morocco. What happened after that?"

He folded his arms and leaned back in his chair. "Bahnini hadn't been as careful as Nazer would have liked. He'd opened a bank account with a gold mine of information that all led back to Nazer. We started looking into several deposits from Kenya, which is how we traced Nazer's training camp there, and it was the first place we searched for you. Once we had those financial records, we were able to track Nazer and his assets in a myriad of ways and shut him down." Julian added a little sugar and took a bite of his porridge.

"Why would Nazer risk having traceable information on that account?" she asked, pouring herself a cup of tea from the set on the tray.

Julian shrugged. "I'm sure that's why he killed the guy. But I don't think he knew how many of his shell corporations and associates were actually known to us. With everything we'd uncovered on Nazer's finances to that point, it wasn't hard to dig up the transactions he'd tried to hide. The bank account filled in a lot of missing pieces." He looked over at her. "And we shut him down the minute we could."

"From what Colt said, he's got a backer." She finished her porridge and took a sip of tea. The hot drink felt good going down her throat. Like a little bit of liquid courage. Maybe if she could help capture Nazer, she could put this behind her once and for all.

"You definitely haven't lost your touch for eavesdropping." Julian leaned over, his elbows resting on the table. "I was going to tell you when you were stronger, you know."

He looked repentant, but she needed to make him understand. "I don't want you deciding when I'm ready to hear things. I don't want anyone deciding anything for me ever again." Her spine straightened. "If I'm going to *heal*, as you put it, I need to know what you know."

"I assume you also heard Colt say there's a hit out on you." He grimaced, as if saying the words was distasteful. "Is it a revenge play, do you think? Or could there be another reason?"

"It has to be a revenge play. What other reason could there be?" She frowned. "They didn't share any of their plans with me. Trying new ways to learn my secrets kept them busy."

An expression of pain flitted over Julian's face, but he wiped it away quickly and leaned closer. "Are you sure? Maybe you overheard something, but didn't realize the significance. It doesn't make sense that he'd come after you now. What does he stand to gain?"

"I have no idea. I didn't see Nazer often, really. I mostly dealt with Saif." His hateful laugh echoed through her mind, and she shuddered.

"But you did see Nazer?" Julian asked gently. He took a sip of tea, keeping his eyes on her as he did.

"A few times. More frequently early on." Thanks to the drugs used when they moved her, some of her memories were hazy. "They mostly wanted to know about you." And when she hadn't answered . . .

Julian closed his eyes. "Z, I'm so sorry."

The Capture

Zaya shook her head. "I can't focus on that right now." She twisted in her chair, enjoying the feeling of being able to analyze the situation with the possibility of figuring out obscure motives and fighting back. Doing something to bring Nazer al-Raimi down felt good. "So you think I might know something damaging to Nazer, and that's why he's put a hit out on me?"

"It's a possibility." Julian leaned back, putting his teacup down on the table. "But he could also be angry you got away. Either way, we have to be careful."

"*I* have to be careful," she clarified.

Julian's hand covered hers. "He's coming after *us* and I won't leave you."

The look in his eyes was intense, and every nerve ending in her fingers and arm charged at his touch. She pulled her hand away and busied herself finishing her drink. "Who knew about your stop at Camp Bastion?"

"Not many people." He furrowed his brow. "My team. The Afghan army liaison that rented it. A few of my sources at MI6 and one from Comm Headquarters."

Zaya wrinkled her nose. "I can understand having a source at Communication Headquarters. They're second to none in analyzing threats and data, but I thought you cut ties with MI6. Who do you have as a source at Vauxhall Cross? Is anyone still speaking to you there after you broke off to form Griffin Force?"

Julian gave her a half-grin. "I charmed my way back into some good graces."

"I can believe that," Zaya muttered to herself. "Anyone who was still upset that you took some of their top agents for Griffin Force?"

"Maybe." He rubbed his jaw. "I didn't think so, but I'm running out of explanations for how Nazer knows so much about our operations. Not enough to stop us, per se, but enough not to get caught."

"And you have no idea who the mole could be?" She crossed her legs. This was just like old times. Talking through a case. Brainstorming. For the first time in months, she felt a shade of familiarity calling to her from her old life.

"Obviously I need to do a little digging. Spread some of my charm around." He sat back in his chair. "But the first thing on the agenda is taking care of you."

She flicked her hand in the air, as if to wave away his words. "I refuse to be an agenda item."

"You're my favorite agenda item." A light shone in his eyes when he looked at her. She turned away.

"I won't be on anyone's agenda now. I'm found. I'm home. You can check that off your list." Fiddling with the handle of her teacup, she took a breath and let it out slowly. Julian was still, and she could feel his eyes on her. Raising her chin, she met his gaze.

"I want to discuss where we go from here, Z." He talked slowly, and his words were earnest, as if he wanted her to really listen. But before she could say anything, a knock sounded at the door.

"Give us a minute," Julian called out.

"Chief Sinclair is coming up the drive. Do you want us to detain him?" Colt sounded calm, even with the message he was delivering.

Julian uttered a soft curse before he crossed the room and threw open the door. "What's William doing here? I told him to stay away for now."

Zaya limped over to stand next to him, but Julian didn't let her get far. "Stay up here while I talk to him, okay? He's going to want a debrief . . ."

His voice trailed off, but Zaya finished the thought for him. "That you don't think I'm ready for." She took a deep breath. "And you're right. I'm not."

He bent and nonchalantly dropped a kiss on her forehead, like he'd done a thousand times before. *Before.* Her life seemed to be firmly divided into the Before and After and she didn't know how she felt about that. Could that change, or would it always be that way?

Julian lightly squeezed her shoulders. "No one will get near you until you're ready." And then he turned and was gone.

Zaya put a hand to her middle. Her emotions were so torn. There was so much comfort in the familiarity of Julian, but at the same time, that closeness made her nervous. She slowly moved back to her chair by the window, trying to gather her thoughts. The garden outside was mostly barren, except for a few hardy flowers that still bloomed and some leaves clinging to the trees. Inside she felt like one of those leaves, trying to cling

92

onto what she knew and combine it with what she'd already survived, before she dropped into an unknown future.

Wishing she could pace, and knowing she needed a distraction, Zaya grabbed the medical bag off the floor and tried to rebandage her feet. She hadn't taken a good look at her wounds before, and her stomach twisted as she bent to examine her feet. Both soles had white crisscross scars from the caning, mixed with the redness and a more recent wound that hadn't healed. Her left foot was definitely worse than her right. It looked like minced beef. She quickly covered it with the bandage and did the best she could to bind it.

When she finished, all there was to do was sit and listen. Doors opening and closing in the house below were the only sounds to break the silence in her room. What if Chief Sinclair demanded to see her? Forced her to relive every moment of captivity? The thought squeezed the breath from her lungs. The specter of Saif and what she'd suffered was too close. Zaya put her hands over her ears and drew her legs up underneath her, resting her cheek on her knees. All the feelings she'd had of finding a bit of her old self fled. Who was she fooling? She'd never find that woman again. Her hands slid from her ears, and she covered her head. Tears clogged her throat, but wouldn't release.

"Julian," she whispered.

He deserves so much more than me.

If nothing else, she'd proved that by hiding up here instead of facing the MI6 director. She wasn't strong or capable.

The Capture

The woman Julian loved and remembered had transformed in a dirty cell to someone unrecognizable. She opened her eyes and stared at the door, wishing she had the courage to walk through it. To do something besides cower in her room.

And with that thought, the tears came again.

CHAPTER EIGHT

Julian hated to leave Zaya when she was vulnerable, but he had to find out why the British Secret Intelligence Chief would be visiting him. He'd told Chief Sinclair—William to those who knew him best—to give him a few days. Had something important come up with Nazer's case?

He strode through the empty hallways, his steps silent on the carpeted floor. Even with his efforts to make the house somewhat livable, it still seemed empty. Taking a breath, he walked into the front room, where William stood in front of the stone fireplace.

He turned at Julian's entrance and held up a hand. "I know you said to give you time, but we've had a development. I need to talk to Zaya immediately."

Julian folded his arms. His first instinct was to say absolutely not, but he needed to hear William out. He needed to stay objective when it came to Zaya, or at the very least *appear* to be objective. "What's the development?"

"Nazer is here in England, and I think he's coming for her." He paused, as if to give Julian a moment to process that. "Two birdwatchers were shot near Chichester Harbour this morning, which wouldn't have put us on the case, but then investigators found a small boat crew on the beach, all dead, killed execution-style."

"I still don't see why MI6 would be on that. Seems like a matter for the local police." Julian clenched his jaw. Nazer was known for execution-style killings. So were most terrorists, gang members, and serial killers. But at the grim look on William's face, the last shred of hope in Julian's gut died.

"One of the birdwatchers survived and positively identified Nazer as the shooter." William sat down in the overstuffed chair next to the fireplace, as if the weight he carried was too heavy to bear standing up. "He's had a hit out on you for a long time, but that hasn't touched you in England, yet the moment you bring Zaya back, Nazer appears on English soil? No, there has to be a reason he'd come for her. She knows something."

Julian sat down in the matching chair. They now had confirmation that Nazer hadn't been left behind in Afghanistan. How would Zaya handle that? How could he protect her? He shook his head and focused on William. "She told me she didn't see Nazer much beyond her first days in captivity." He looked over at William. "And I think we have a bigger problem. Nazer found us pretty quickly at Camp Bastion. We nearly didn't get out of there. Now he's followed us to England? He's got to have an inside source." His words were clipped, his frustration showing.

William raised his eyebrows, unfazed by his sharpness. "How many people knew you were there?"

"Not many. Nazer has to have a mole in the intelligence community." Julian ran a hand over his face, the stress from the last two days catching up to him. Would they ever be able to leave Nazer behind? "I've got my team looking into a few things for me."

"You know I've been investigating a possible mole myself. Let me know if your people find anything." William hesitated for a minute, then steepled his fingers over his lap. "How is she, Julian?"

He thought of the scene he'd witnessed this morning, the wild fear in her eyes when she woke up and thought she was still a prisoner. "As well as can be expected. They found her in squalid conditions, locked in a cell. She was caned—often, from the look of her scars, and she has an infection in one foot from the untreated wounds she suffered. She needs time to heal emotionally and physically."

William folded his hands in his lap. "I know you don't like it, but I won't take long with her. You know I'll be gentle." William started to stand, but Julian waved him back, his jaw set.

"No one is going to talk to her today. Or tomorrow. Not yet." He was firm on that. Zaya wouldn't be put through a debrief until she'd had a chance to adjust.

William stood up and used his height advantage over a sitting Julian to look down at him. "Nazer is on British soil. Zaya is the only link we have to him. I'm going to talk to her. It's a matter of national security to get him locked down as soon as possible. Remember his attack on us last year? If she has any idea what he's doing here or where he's going, I need to know."

"If you really think he's really coming after her, then you know where he's headed." Julian stood, too, toe-to-toe, but with a slight height advantage of an inch or so. "Besides, with the entire staff of MI6 at your disposal, you have other options. Put some agents on overtime to track him or run down leads or something, because no one gets near Zaya until I say."

"You're not her keeper. I think she should decide who can debrief her. Or are you afraid of what she'll say?" William pinned him with his gaze. He might have been shorter than Julian, but he made up for it in presence. Which was part of what made him a good intelligence chief, since people could be intimidated with just a pointed glance.

But not Julian. Not anymore.

"Zaya will be debriefed when she tells me she's ready and not a moment before." Julian took a step back, needing to disengage before he did or said something he'd regret.

William mirrored his step. "And by then, Nazer could have hurt a lot of innocent people."

It was a strange dance they were doing, but Julian wasn't going to compromise with Zaya's well-being. "You can't put that on Zaya. She doesn't know where he is, and doesn't know any of his plans. Use MI6 resources. Find another way."

William snorted. "Why put anyone else on this when she could tell us everything we need to know? One conversation. That's all I'm asking for."

Julian stepped closer again, anger charging through him. One conversation with William could be worse than the emotional torture she'd already endured. They couldn't ask her to relive it all just yet when she was stretched so thin trying to acclimate to freedom. "You have no idea what you're asking for, what she's been through. She's fragile and needs our support, not an interrogation."

William put up his hand. "You're right," he conceded. "But you have to admit, Nazer could be planning another attack on English soil. Sooner rather than later. We need to be sure Zaya didn't inadvertently hear something. Figure out why Nazer is coming after her."

"What about a compromise?" Julian tried to relax and let the tension seep out of him. "I'll ask her a few questions when I can see she's ready, and then give you a report."

William was quiet for a moment, watching Julian. "You're too close to the investigation. To her. You need to let someone else in, even if it's just to observe."

"I'm not sure I know what you mean." Julian hadn't discussed his feelings for Zaya with anyone, least of all William.

"Oh, don't play coy with me. Before she was kidnapped, you two could finish each other's sentences, and then you were relentless in searching for her. While I know you would do a lot for your friends and colleagues, I've never seen you so driven." He shrugged. "It's okay to love someone, you know. And in our business, love doesn't come easily, so I was happy for both of you."

Julian tilted his head in acknowledgment, but didn't verbally confirm anything. "So, you don't think I can objectively question her?"

William shook his head. "You won't be able to push her."

"I won't need to push her. Zaya wants to help. All I'm saying is, she needs a second to breathe, that's all." And to feel safe. Hopefully Mrs. Finch would be able to make some headway in helping her too.

William let out a long sigh. "We don't have time to wait."

"We'll make the time." This was one instance when Julian wouldn't back down. Zaya deserved that.

The door opened, and they both looked over as Colt and Jake entered the room. "Julian, when you have a minute, Augie needs to talk to you about something." Colt surveyed William. "Anything we can do to help the situation in here?"

"Chief Sinclair was just leaving," Julian said, stepping toward the doorway.

"I'm interested in hearing what Augie needs to talk to you about," William said, looking from Julian to Colt.

Julian folded his arms. "You know the deal, William. If we get actionable intel, we'll share it with you. Other than that, I have to keep things separate. Then everyone is on the straight and narrow."

William shook his head. "We'll both be tracking down Nazer, and I'll be working around the clock. I suspect you will as well, but if we don't make headway, we'll have to come back to Zaya." William gave him a pointed stare, then walked through the doorway.

"Be prepared to get the same answer you got today," Julian called after him. He followed William out and glanced up the stairs as they gained the hallway. Was she all right? Who was with her? He couldn't hustle William out of here fast enough so he could check on her.

William's eyes followed his as he put on his coat. "You can't shield her forever."

"Watch me." He escorted William to the front door and waited until he was in his car. That hadn't gone well. William had some patience, but it would run out. Julian needed a contingency plan.

When William's car was going down the drive, Colt appeared at his side. "What was that about?"

"We got confirmation that Nazer is in England. He killed a boat crew and shot two birdwatchers. One survived to positively ID him. Of course, Sinclair wants to question Zaya to see if she knows anything about what he's got planned." Julian's voice was curt as he gave a summary of his conversation with

101

William. He started back toward the stairs as he talked, anxious to get back to Zaya.

Colt stayed beside him. "And you don't want to let William talk to her about it because . . . ?" The question hung in the air.

"She's wounded. I'm not going to turn her over to an interrogation the second she gets back to England." That would feel like another betrayal to both of them. He might not have been able to protect her the first time, but he wouldn't let her down again.

"Well, if Nazer is here, we need to make a few changes to our security, for both the house and for Zaya. The sooner the better."

Julian stopped on the stairs. Colt was right. They needed to take care of their security issues before he went back to Zaya. With one last glance up the stairs, he turned around and went back down. "Let's meet in the conference room. Then Augie can update us and we can draw up a battle plan." If Julian had anything to say about it, Nazer wouldn't ever get close to Zaya again.

They walked down the hall to the makeshift "conference" room, which was a beautiful old library, complete with shelves tall enough to need a rolling ladder. The smell of paper and bindings was oddly comforting to Julian and he took a deep breath as he stepped inside. He needed to think clearly in order to help Zaya. William had accused him of being too close, and while that might be true, he was determined not to let that affect his plans for Zaya's safety.

Julian sat behind the desk, and Colt, Jake, Brenna, and Augie took up the chairs in front of him. "Where are Nate and Mya?" Julian asked Jake.

"Nate's on security detail. Mya'll be here shortly. Her father isn't feeling well, and she's been on the phone with her sister, trying to figure out what they're going to do for his care." Jake settled back in his chair. When Julian first met Jake, he'd seemed intense and more than a little restless, as if he had something to prove. Since he'd come to Griffin Force and gotten engaged to Mya, he'd become sharper, as if life had come into focus for him.

Once everyone's attention was on him, Julian turned to Augie. If anyone could pick up Nazer's trail electronically, he could. The man was the most brilliant computer hacker/analyst Julian had ever come across. Griffin Force was lucky to have him.

"Okay, what's your news?" Julian wanted to cut right to the chase and start forming a plan. The more prepared he was, the safer Zaya would be.

"I've been backtracing all the links we've found to Nazer's account, going over everything three and four times and I found something. There are regular transactions with a set amount of money, run through several shell corporations, at the same time each month. And they were always deposited in the same bank in England. I'm not sure how we missed it, but once I connected the dots, it was easy to see the pattern." Augie looked around the room triumphantly. "I think Nazer may have a biological child here in England and he's paying child support."

Augie's voice echoed through Julian's mind, and stunned silence reigned in the room.

Colt was the first to recover. "That's a pretty big stretch. Just because he's making regular deposits here doesn't necessarily mean they're child support."

"Once I had the bank name and the transaction dates, I hacked into the bank's surveillance feed. And that led me to this woman." He turned his laptop screen around and showed a picture of a woman with a young boy. "Caroline Alden."

Julian stared at the grainy picture. She looked like any other English girl he'd see on the street, blonde, dressed in jeans and a t-shirt, holding her son in her arms. Was that Nazer's child she held? If he squinted, he could see a resemblance. "Where does she live?"

"Woolwich." Augie pushed his glasses back up on his nose and turned his computer screen back to face himself. "Ms. Alden was a music teacher at a British primary school in Bahrain. One of Nazer's nephews attended there, and I think that's where they met. She returned to Britain before the school year ended and had her baby here."

Julian paused, trying to absorb the ramifications of the possibility of Nazer having a son here. "It's all circumstantial, though."

"Circumstantial, but compelling," Augie said, his eyebrows raised.

"I wonder if she knows who he is and what he really does?" If Julian were a betting man, he would say no.

Brenna shook her head. "How could she not know? His face was plastered all over the news after the attacks in London last year. But if Nazer's in England, she needs to know to protect her son."

"And if he's here to visit the boy, that could be our opportunity." Jake sat forward, every muscle in his body tense, as if he was ready to spring into action right then. It was easy to see he was already formulating a possible plan to capture Nazer. "We could be watching and grab him when he does."

"Go on the offensive, instead of waiting for him to find us? I like that idea." Colt looked around the room, as if to gauge the reaction of everyone else. "I could take a couple of us to Ms. Alden's house to wait for Nazer, and the rest of you can stay here with Zaya."

"Splitting the team might leave Zaya vulnerable," Julian said quietly. "And we're only speculating that he would take time out to visit his child. Maybe his mission is to find and kill Zaya, which means that our attention should be here with her, and making this house a fortress."

"We could call in Sinclair. Team up with him to cover both bases," Jake said. "He's just as anxious to get Nazer as we are."

Julian shook his head. "Someone in intelligence is leaking our plans. Nazer would know we're coming. Whatever we do, until we find the mole, we have to keep everything amongst ourselves."

Brenna nodded, her expression thoughtful. "I'll put out some discreet inquiries to my contacts. We know Nazer's back is to the wall with so many of his assets frozen. His options are dwindling. Someone has to know something about the mole. Once we have a name, we can shut his partner down and, without him, Nazer knows his days as a free man are over."

"Keep me updated." Julian stood. "I'm going to check on Zaya. Colt, you make up new security rotations and, Augie, keep digging." He gave the computer tech a grateful glance. "Thanks for all you do. We couldn't have gotten this far without you."

Augie flushed at the praise, the redness on his face matching his hair. "Anytime, Commander. We're close to capturing him. I can feel it."

Julian nodded and opened the library door. He paused and looked back at his team. They'd all found a purpose in working to bring down Nazer al-Raimi. Jake had studied Nazer for years and thwarted at least two terrorist attacks in America. His focus had been almost as intense as Julian's, and they'd destroyed a lot of Nazer's empire together. Brenna had been undercover in Nazer's top lieutenant's household and nearly been killed, and Mya had almost lost her sister in one of Nazer's attacks. They'd all been touched irrevocably by trying to bring him down, but somehow, the man always seemed to slink under a new rock and rebuild. Griffin Force had been relentless, but after chasing him for so long, all Julian wanted now was to see Nazer suffer for what he'd done.

He walked down the hall and headed for the stairs. Zaya had paid a heavy price for her involvement in fighting Nazer and his terrorist organization, and ultimately Julian had, too. Now, though, his personal and professional life had blurred. He needed to protect Zaya from further harm. He also had to put Nazer away. But when it came down to it, which was the greater priority?

Stopping outside the door of Zaya's bedroom, Julian could hear voices from inside. He paused. Who was she talking to?

"Don't," Zaya plainly said, loud enough to be heard through the door.

The pain in her voice had him inside the room in seconds. She was standing near the door, as if she was preparing to leave. He gave her a once-over to make sure she was okay, then in relief, reached out and pulled her to him. "What's going on?"

Zaya stiffened in his arms as Mrs. Finch approached them. "Zaya, can I speak to you alone? Please? Just for another moment."

She took a step toward them, but Zaya pushed away from him and bolted through the open door. Mrs. Finch moved to follow, but Julian blocked the way, folding his arms across his chest. "You're not going anywhere until you tell me what just happened in this room."

CHAPTER NINE

Zaya hobbled down the stairs, anxious to get away from everyone in her room. She stumbled on the second to last step and almost landed in a heap at the bottom, but caught herself just in time. Cursing her injuries, she held onto the railing for a moment and caught her breath. There were voices coming from a room down the hall, and she wasn't in the mood to talk to anyone, so she went the opposite way toward the large front door. With one glance back, she opened it and walked out onto the porch. The air was crisp, but not cold, and it felt good on her cheeks. Closing her eyes, she sucked in a lungful.

Assessing her options, and the fact that her left foot throbbed, she moved to the furniture on the porch. She smiled a bit, looking at the placement. Every wicker chair and couch was backed against the wall, facing outward, like a platoon taking a defensive position waiting for the enemy. She pulled one out and sat down, then lifted her aching foot. The bandage was red, which meant she'd probably opened up her wound. But she couldn't stay in that room with Mrs. Finch anymore.

Mrs. Finch, Zaya thought bitterly. *What rubbish.*

The woman was more than a friendly houseguest, having announced to Zaya that she was really Dr. Finch, specializing in mental health and cognitive restructuring for military veterans suffering from PTSD. Why hadn't Julian or the doctor been up front and given the woman a proper introduction right away? Did Julian really think Zaya was so emotionally fragile that she needed round-the-clock care?

The front door creaked open and she clenched her fists. If that was Julian, she'd walk away, leaving a trail of bloody footprints behind if she had to. He'd have to give up eventually and let her be, right? But it wasn't Julian. Brenna poked her head out the door.

"I thought I heard someone come out here," Brenna said, walking over to join her. "Can I sit for a minute? It's been a busy morning."

Zaya nodded, glad for the distraction. Brenna had a calmness about her that Zaya was drawn to, and she needed that right now. "What's going on?"

Brenna leaned forward, her elbows on her knees. "We got confirmation that Nazer is in England, so we've been trying to figure out if he's coming after you, or if he has something else in mind."

Zaya folded her hands, grateful that Brenna was offering information, treating her like part of the team. She wanted more. "Do you think he'd attack London again?" After his extensive strikes last year, that seemed unlikely. Wouldn't he move on to a different location?

"You know how hard terrorists like him are to predict." Brenna sat back. "How are you feeling?"

"Angry. Worried. Happy. I've got every emotion you can think of running through me right now." Zaya let out a breath. "I'm on sensory overload, to tell you the truth." She squinted and looked down over the driveway. "After being in the dark for so long, daylight is disorienting. Having food available to me any time I want is hard to wrap my head around. It's like I'm still waiting for someone to snatch my freedom away again."

Brenna was silent for a moment, as if weighing her words. "Would it help to talk it out with someone?"

"Isn't that why Julian hired Dr. Finch? So I could have a shrink at my beck and call?" It burned that he'd had a doctor waiting without giving her a chance to see if she could handle things on her own, or if she even wanted treatment.

"You sound upset about that." Brenna shifted in her chair so she could face Zaya. "You know he just wants you to have all the tools you need. That's why he's spared no expense with this house, Dr. Finch, your protection." Brenna looked at her, a hint of reproach in her eyes. "He nearly worked himself to death trying to find you, and I've watched him be eaten up with guilt when he failed again and again. He's being a little overprotective, but he has good reason. He loves you, Z."

Zaya wanted to cover her face and her ears. How selfish she must sound. Brenna was right, but that didn't make the truth easier to hear. "I'm sorry. Like I said, I'm on sensory overload and feeling a little out of control and I hate that. Having my decisions made for me is driving me crazy, and that's what I need Julian to understand."

Before Brenna could answer, Julian pushed the door open and joined them on the porch, his hands stuffed into his pants pockets. "Hey."

Brenna stood with a small smile. "Maybe I'll go see if I can find some more of those scones. Would you like one, Zaya?"

She shook her head. "Not right now, but thank you." Her stomach tightened at the prospect of having to face Julian. Had he overheard what she'd said?

"I'll see you later." She brushed past Julian and went inside.

"May I sit?" Julian asked, his brown eyes watchful, assessing. Was he worried she'd attack him? Run away?

"Okay." She moved her knees so he could get by her, folding his larger frame into the chair Brenna had vacated next to hers. He scooted forward so he was nearly touching her. His bulk made the porch seem smaller, and her heart sped up. She took a breath and counted to three before she let it out. This was Julian. He would never hurt her or use his strength against her.

"Mrs. Finch told me what happened." He didn't look at her, just stared out at the trees lining the long driveway.

"Why didn't you tell me she's a therapist?" Zaya asked softly. "Why couldn't you trust me with even that small bit of information?"

"You were so sick yesterday, and this morning, there wasn't a good opportunity for introductions before I got called downstairs." He moved his hand closer, and when she didn't pull away, he enveloped her fingers with his. "She's the best in the country and has helped hundreds of veterans process what happened to them in the field."

"Were you so sure I'd be damaged enough to need twenty-four hour care from a therapist?" The heat from his hand sent a zing of warmth up her arm. "Didn't you want to wait a bit to see if I could handle things on my own?"

"I wanted to have a contingency plan in place, to be ready with anything you might need. If you don't want her, then she'll go back to her day job in Surrey. If you do, she's being paid handsomely to be here." Julian gave her hand a squeeze. "Even the strongest women can use a bit of help now and again."

Zaya sighed, the anger seeping out of her. "Thank you." She leaned back in her chair. "No more surprises, though, okay? I need to be in charge of my life again. I can't . . . I can't let anyone make decisions for me."

"I'm sorry it came across that way. I promise to make sure you're informed." His thumb lightly stroked the back of her hand now. She wanted to close her eyes and enjoy the pleasure that small movement awakened in her, but she knew that wouldn't lead anywhere she could emotionally go. Straightening, she pulled away and changed the subject.

"Brenna said that Nazer is in England. What do you know?" Zaya clenched her fist, missing his comforting warmth already and willing herself not to reach out for him again. She couldn't send him mixed messages by leaning on him one moment and withdrawing the next, no matter how much she wanted to let herself give in to his familiarity.

Julian ran a hand over his face. "Augie found evidence that Nazer might have a biological child living in England."

"What?" Her jaw nearly hit the floor. That was the last thing she'd expected. "Has the mother been on MI6's radar at all?"

"No, it's something Augie uncovered on his own. But now we're wondering whether he's here to see the child, or if he's coming after us." He leaned closer. "My gut tells me that the child is a distraction. He put a hit out on you, so it's clear to me where he'll be heading."

"But coming after me still makes no sense beyond getting revenge for my rescue. His focus has always been you." She took a deep breath. "Sinclair doesn't believe it's a revenge play, though, does he?"

"No, he thinks you know something Nazer is anxious to keep buried." He paused and massaged the back of his neck. "Z, I hate to ask again, but think back. Could there be anything?"

Zaya pulled inside herself. Thoughts of those first days made her shrink, but she forced herself there. The rancid smell. The darkness. The first beating. Nazer had been there for it all, but he hadn't said much beyond questioning her over and over about Julian. After the initial sessions, though, Nazer had taken on more of an observer role, barely speaking, and eventually, he stopped coming.

"He just wanted to know about you and Griffin Force operations, that's all." Her shoulders drooped, wishing she could think of something to help him and the investigation. "I'm sorry."

"You don't have anything to be sorry for." He patted her upper arm and let his hand slide down to intertwine their fingers. "William just wanted to be sure."

They stayed like that for a moment, companionably enjoying birdsong in the trees with a light breeze blowing over them. Zaya hadn't appreciated the outdoors enough before. But her foot was starting to hurt unbearably, and she knew she needed to change the bandage and take some more medicine.

"I'm going to need some help getting back to my room." She spoke softly, unwilling to ruin the moment, but knowing she had to. "I reinjured my foot coming down the stairs."

In the blink of an eye, Julian was on his knees, concern etched in his face as he inspected the blood soaking through her bandage. "We need to take care of this right away." He stood. "Can I carry you back upstairs so you don't put any more pressure on it?"

Zaya's stomach did a little flip at the thought of being in his arms again. Part of her wanted to say she didn't need to be carried and could make it having him at her side while she hopped up the stairs. Instead, she nodded.

The Capture

Julian picked her up and tucked her close to him. She laid her cheek against his chest, listening to his heartbeat. Strong and sure, like he'd always been. He maneuvered through the front door and took her upstairs to her room. Carefully setting her on the bed, he grabbed the medical bag and started taking out supplies. "I'm going to put in a call to Elliott to see what he recommends."

He crouched in front of her and rested her left ankle on his thigh as he took off the soiled bandage. "You should have called me."

"You were a little busy after my shower, so I made do." The words came out more breathless than she cared to admit. His hands were gentle, but efficient as he reapplied the antibiotic ointment and rebandaged it.

"You need to stay off your feet to give them a chance to heal." He held the back of her ankle and set her foot gently on the floor. His tenderness made her heart melt a little more. Before she could reassure him that she'd take better care of it, his gaze turned thoughtful. "What if I gave you some research to do while you recover?"

The idea took her by surprise, but felt exciting and scary at the same time. "What kind of research?"

"Getting more information on Nazer's child and the mother. Being a second pair of eyes for Augie. You might find something he missed." Julian stood, the smile he reserved only for her on his face. "You're the most thorough researcher I know."

How could she resist that? "Get me a laptop." She gingerly pulled her feet onto the bed and leaned against the headboard, unable to keep her grin hidden.

He didn't leave to get her the computer, though, and sat down next to her instead. "What do you really think about Dr. Finch? She's the best in the country, and I think she might be able to help, but I can send her away if you don't want her around."

Zaya dropped her eyes. "No, you're right. It's good she's here. I'm obviously having a bit of trouble readjusting. Getting some help is the right call. And I probably owe her an apology."

"She understands. I can send her up when you're ready. It doesn't even have to be today." Julian lifted her chin. "Things are going to be okay, Z."

Tears pooled in her eyes, and she blinked them away. "I hope so."

His thumb stroked her jaw, and he leaned closer. "It will." She stared into his eyes, but seeing love still there was wondrous, and also frightening. Placing her hand over his, she gently pulled it away.

"Julian, things are complicated." She wanted him to understand how hard this was for her. How much she wanted to trust herself, to trust in the love they'd once shared. But it was just too much to ask of her right now.

"I know." He smiled and ran his hand through his hair. "I'll go get you that laptop."

The Capture

A soft knock at the door came seconds before Brenna and Mya came in. "I hope we're not intruding," Brenna said, an apologetic look on her face. "Whenever I wasn't feeling like myself, my mom would make me a grilled cheese sandwich and a smoothie. I thought the same might help you." She nodded toward the plate and glass she was holding. "And Mya wanted to introduce herself."

Mya's smooth olive complexion and beautiful dark hair made Zaya wish she could pull the covers over her head and hide her own ugliness. Mya hesitated a moment, as if she could read Zaya's mind, but then she stepped forward with a smile. "I've heard so much about you that I feel like I know you already. It's nice to finally meet you in person."

Zaya tilted her head, hearing warmth and sincerity in the other woman's tone, and she relaxed. "I hope they were good things."

"Of course." Mya sat down in the chair. "Although someone mentioned you're a little stubborn. They might have been projecting, though." She gave Julian a sly grin.

"Really?" Zaya's eyes narrowed as she pinned Julian. "*You* called *me* stubborn?"

He held up his hands and backed toward the door. "You know, I'll just go get that laptop. Be right back."

When he was gone, the three women burst out laughing.

"I've never seen Julian so meek." Mya folded her hands in her lap. "But all joking aside, you have an incredible reputation as an operative."

"Thanks." Zaya dipped her head in acknowledgment of the praise. "But I want to hear more about you. How did you get involved with Griffin Force?"

"It's a long story, but basically my father was asked to negotiate a hostage release. Nazer took an American diplomat and my sister, who'd been translating for him." Mya bit her lip. "My father is a complicated man, and I was called in to provide incentive for his cooperation in mediating an exchange. After it was all over and everyone was safe, Julian approached our team about joining Griffin Force. We agreed, and here we are."

"Nazer had your sister?" Zaya shivered. "I'm sorry we have that man in common."

Mya glanced over at Brenna, who was sitting on the side of the bed. "Brenna was inserted into Nazer's top lieutenant's household and had several dealings with him as well. He nearly killed both her and Colt."

The air in the room seemed heavy, and Zaya's breathing slowed as she tried to get more air. Nazer had changed all of their lives.

Brenna tried to lighten the mood. "Well, look on the bright side. Mya fell in love with Jake on that operation, and I got a second chance with Colt. In a way, fighting Nazer brought us together."

Zaya nodded, but her eyes strayed to the closed door Julian had gone through. Her heart ached knowing that there might not be any second chances for them. "At least all your worry and suffering had a happy ending." She turned back to the two women, trying to focus on them. But, inside, she still wished things were different. That they *could* be different.

"Yours did, too," Brenna said, leaning forward. "You're here and safe with us."

"You're right," she said, but the words rang hollow. Thoughts of Julian crowded her mind, her heart wishing for what the life she'd had before, full of light and happiness. She did have a lot to be grateful for, though. She was alive and home. Maybe that had to be enough.

CHAPTER TEN

Julian wasn't surprised when he brought the laptop back to find Zaya chatting with Brenna and Mya as if they were old friends. He debated interrupting—this was the first time he'd truly seen her relax since she'd been back—but in the end, he couldn't resist being with her too.

"What did I miss?" he asked as he set the laptop on the end of the bed.

Zaya looked up at him, a crinkle in her forehead. "They've been catching me up on everything I've missed in the last six months. Did you know fuchsia is making a big comeback?"

Julian shook his head. "I had no idea. But I'm more of a black or camo sort of guy."

Zaya gave him a half-hearted sigh and a smile, her eyes lit with memories. "I remember. And you do look amazing at black-tie events."

Julian's breath hitched, remembering the last black-tie they'd been to. That's where they'd first said I love you. Did she remember? "You didn't look so bad yourself." He'd never forget the royal blue gown that clung to her in all the right places. He cleared his throat. "Did Brenna mention that minimalism is a big thing now? Who knew I was a trendsetter."

"Trendsetter? You're only a minimalist because you never stayed anywhere long enough to have more than two boxes of belongings. You like living by the seat of your pants." She grinned up at him.

"Hey, I'm not the only one," Julian protested. "I don't recall seeing any embroidered tea towels in your London flat."

Zaya's smile vanished. "You know, I hadn't even thought about my flat." All the lightheartedness that had permeated the room turned melancholy. "My lease would have run out by now and all my things put in the dustbin."

Julian wished he'd never mentioned it, but was glad he'd taken care of her belongings. "I packed everything and stored the boxes in my parents' attic." He shifted, remembering how hard that day was. Packing her clothes and books felt like giving up on her. "We can go get them when you're better—and visit Milo at the same time."

Her face brightened a little at that. "Milo's still alive?"

"Who's Milo?" Brenna asked, looking between them.

"A spoiled, lazy cat that loves all the attention my parents give him." Julian turned to face Brenna and Mya. "I had this stray hanging around my flat for weeks, acting like he owned the place. He was always waiting for me when I got home, no matter what time of day or night, so I started talking to him. That led to feeding him, and before I knew it, we were getting on so famously, we just claimed each other."

"When did you give him to your parents?" Brenna asked.

"A few months ago. I was out of town and the poor bloke needed food and companionship. My parents have some property in Kent, and Milo has been happy as a clam out there. My mum tells me he might even have a lady friend or two now." Julian leaned against the footboard of the bed. "I'm not sure he even misses me."

"Of course he misses you," Zaya said, adamantly. "You were his world and always will be." Her words hung in the air, and she flushed. Julian hoped that splash of color in her face meant she was thinking the same in regard to him. "How are your parents?"

"Fine. They'll be anxious to see you." Julian thought back to how quickly she'd taken to his mother. Zaya's own mother had died in a car accident when she was young, and she'd never known her father. Her grandmother raised her and died shortly after Zaya joined Griffin Force. When they first met, Zaya had seemed so self-contained, like she didn't need to have places to go for holidays, but after seeing her with his parents, a more vulnerable side had come out that showed how much she missed having a family. It had endeared her to them all.

The best part of this whole conversation, though, was the fact that she was responding to him, even if it was only tiny moments here and there. Every second of it made his heart feel lighter.

"I'm anxious to see them, too" Zaya said, her eyes soft.

He cleared his throat, the image in his mind of her at his parents' house making him want to take her there today and wrap her up in all of their love. The timing wasn't right yet, though. "I put a call in to Elliott, so he should be here shortly. Charlie's doing much better and is going to be released today."

"She was the most seriously injured at Camp Bastion," Mya supplied. "I'm glad you guys were all able to get out of there."

"Do we have any other intel on the mole who leaked our location?" Brenna said, sitting forward.

"No, not yet. Augie is running down a few more leads. It's a short list of people who knew we were there." Julian glanced at Zaya. "I've asked Zaya to help with some of the research. We can use her expertise."

"Definitely." Brenna stood up and smoothed her blouse. "I need to go check on some of my own irons in the fire. I have a conference call coming in a few minutes that I need to prepare for."

"Anything I should know about?" Julian asked, trying to keep his voice casual. Brenna was one of the best for gathering information. She had a network of informants she'd cultivated over the years that always seemed to come through for them.

"Not yet. I'll let you know when something pans out." She walked to the door, and Mya followed her lead. "I hope we can finish our catch-up session later. We didn't even get to all the celebrity gossip of who's together and who's broken up."

"Does she even want to know those things?" Mya said with a roll of her eyes. "If you wait another month or two, they'll all probably be back together. Hollywood is fickle like that."

"Maybe we can pick a movie or two that's come out in the last six months," Zaya said cautiously. "I wouldn't mind catching up on that."

"Deal. There've been some great ones lately. Are you more of an action or romance kind of girl?" Mya asked.

Julian tensed. An action movie might trigger painful emotions. She used to love all the romantic chick flicks, so hopefully she chose that.

"Let's find a comedy," Zaya said finally. "I want something to make me laugh."

"I know the perfect one," Brenna said with a nod. "I'll see what I can do about having it streamed here." She turned toward Julian. "Did you set up Netflix?"

"No," he said slowly. He'd been too wrapped up in getting her here. "We're trying to stay untraceable, remember?"

"No matter. I'm sure Augie can fix us up." She winked at Zaya. "See you later."

"Later," Mya called as she left with a wave.

After they left, the room was quiet. Zaya fiddled with the blankets a bit before she lifted her eyes to Julian. "They seem really nice."

"They're great at what they do, too. Brenna's one of my finest undercover agents. Well, she was," he amended. "She had to blow her cover to get Colt out. She's been partnering with him on intel gathering ever since."

"Do you think she'll ever go back in the field?" Zaya asked softly. Was she asking for herself, or was this still about Brenna?

"It'll depend on the team needs, I suppose, and where her talents fit best without putting her in danger." Julian sat down on the edge of the bed. "You may not think it's feasible right now, and I know it's way too soon, but there is still a place for you on Griffin Force if you want it."

Her eyes shone with tears before she dropped her gaze back to the bed. "I don't know." She fidgeted with the laptop and then opened it. "There are so many things to consider."

Dr. Finch appeared in the doorway. "You know, Zaya, I'd like to help you consider all of your options. I'm sorry we got off on such a bad foot, and I'd like to remedy that if I can."

"Dr. Finch." The words came out on a sigh as Zaya looked up. "I owe you an apology for how I behaved before."

The doctor waved her hand in the air, as if brushing her words away. "I understand. I should have introduced myself as a doctor right away. We had such an abrupt first meeting, and the 'Mrs.' just popped out. I should have corrected it."

"It's fine." Zaya said. She tilted her head and shot a quick glance at Julian before coming back to Dr. Finch. "I don't know if I'm ready to talk about whether I could ever come back to Griffin Force, but the fact is, I could use your help sorting through some other things."

"I'll go see how close Elliott is," Julian said, taking her words as his hint to make himself scarce. "I'll come check on you in a little while."

Before he could stand, she took his hand and squeezed his fingers. "Thank you," she murmured.

Julian squeezed back and got up to leave. Before he went out the door, he looked back. Dr. Finch was settling herself in the chair next to the bed. Zaya didn't look tense, only intent. Gladness surged through him that he'd done something right. Having Dr. Finch here would turn out to be a good thing, maybe even something that could help smooth Zaya's healing process.

He took a deep breath and headed downstairs to the kitchen, making sure the door shut quietly behind him. Maybe he could get some lunch going for them while she talked to Dr. Finch. He knew they had to keep Zaya's diet simple until her body adjusted to regular meals again, but surely a cucumber sandwich would be easy on her system. They'd been her favorite.

Colt was rummaging in the refrigerator when Julian made it to the kitchen. "Find anything good?" Julian asked as he opened the fridge wider and peered in himself.

"Fixings for a cheese and pickle sandwich," Colt said, holding up the pickle jar triumphantly.

Julian wrinkled his nose. "That sounds terrible."

"Don't knock it 'til you try it," Colt answered, getting the bread out. "How's Zaya?"

"Better. Mya and Brenna went up to get acquainted, and I think that really lifted her spirits." Julian gave up on making anything until Colt was done with his lunch and sat at the table instead. "They were catching her up on everything she's missed in the last six months. Fashion news, celebrities, stuff like that." He put his chin in his hand. "She never seemed to care about that stuff before. Her life revolved around her work, but maybe being distracted by things that don't have anything to do with what happened to her is what she needs right now."

"Is she sleeping?" Colt licked some pickle juice running down the side of his hand.

"Dr. Finch is with her." Julian leaned on his elbows. "Maybe if she can verbalize her experiences with someone, it'll be like extracting the poison."

Colt joined him at the table. "The things she went through will never leave her, Julian, you know that. She can only learn how to deal with the scars and try to live as normally as possible."

Julian ran a hand over his face. "You don't know how badly I want to erase the last six months for her."

"I know. Believe me, there were things Brenna went through that I wish she hadn't. But she got through it. Zaya will, too. Wait and see." He took a bite of his sandwich, a little pickle juice running down his chin, which he wiped away.

"Thanks, man," Julian said, turning to face Colt. "Thanks for getting her out and helping keep me sane through this whole thing."

"You're a great boss," Colt said as he nudged Julian's shoulder. "And you've turned into a good friend."

Jake came in through the back door, wiping sweat from his forehead. He was the picture of what a former U.S. Navy SEAL looked like—military haircut and enough muscle to make anyone think twice about engaging him in hand-to-hand combat. He was good at his job, laser-like in his focus and professional. But he had a sense of justice that pushed him to go the extra mile when it came to helping people and tracking down Nazer before he hurt anyone else.

"How come Nate and I are the only ones working around here?" Jake complained as he joined them at the table.

Colt pushed the other half of his sandwich toward Jake. "Want a cheese and pickle sandwich?"

Jake grimaced. "I'd rather eat an MRE."

"Ouch," Julian said with a laugh. "I can make a couple of cucumber sandwiches if you like."

Jake shook his head. "Doesn't anyone like a plain PB&J around here?" He got up and went over to the cupboards to look around. His second try, he turned around with a jar of peanut butter in hand. "At least someone has good taste."

He quickly made himself a sandwich and one for Julian as well. "So, what's our new plan of action?"

"Thanks for the sandwich," he said, as he reached for the plate. "I think we should up our perimeter checks, make sure we've got enough surveillance that no one is getting on or off this property without us knowing. And have someone with Zaya at all times."

"She doesn't seem the type to want a babysitter," Jake said before he took a bite.

"It's not babysitting. It's a precaution." How could he ever explain the near-panic that rushed through his system whenever he thought of her alone or afraid? That he wanted to put a permanent perimeter around her that would somehow keep her safe for the rest of her life. The feelings were intense sometimes. Maybe it might be a good idea for him to have a few conversations with Dr. Finch himself.

"The rotation schedule is set," Colt said. "And I have first watch."

"I saw that, thanks." Julian stretched his legs out. "From what I heard upstairs, it sounds like we're all going to stay in and watch a movie tonight. How long has it been since we did anything like that?"

"I don't think we've *ever* done anything like that," Jake said. "I'm up for a night in, though."

"If I'm taking first watch, you'll have second and miss the movie," Colt added, with a smirk. "Maybe we can rope Nate into taking a double shift. Or rope Elliott into second watch."

Julian looked at his watch. "I wonder where Elliott is. He told me he'd be here half an hour ago." He picked up his phone and dialed Elliott's number, but it went straight to voicemail. A shiver of unease went down his spine. "That's odd."

"What?" Colt asked, giving him an alert glance.

"Elliott's not answering."

"Maybe his phone's dead," Jake offered, always the practical one.

"Or maybe Nazer found us." Julian pushed back from the table. "You two stay here with Zaya. I'm going to look for Elliott."

CHAPTER ELEVEN

Zaya had moved to the chair to talk to Dr. Finch. For some reason, she just felt more powerful sitting there than in a bed. She was nervous. What if she couldn't talk about what happened? What if Dr. Finch wanted details from her she wasn't ready to give?

Dr. Finch took the chair next to her. She smiled and sat back, as if they were two old friends taking tea on a Sunday. "Zaya, before we start, there are a few things I want to say to preface the work you have ahead of you."

Zaya's stomach twisted, and her heart rate picked up. What if she couldn't do it? Maybe this was the best her life would ever be, carrying around a panicky feeling with her everywhere she went.

Dr. Finch met her eyes. "I think you've already realized that you're not the same person you were. Your body is reacting to things differently, you're dealing with your emotions differently, and you probably feel alone, even though an entire team is downstairs who want what's best for you."

Zaya couldn't help it; the tears started to fall the moment those words penetrated her mind. "Yes," she whispered. "I've seen that."

"You're still in survival mode. I know what happened this morning with the tray upset you, but your body is on high alert for danger. That's why you're reacting this way. It's instinct after what you've been through. If we continue, there are several ways we can reduce that feeling and help you cope." Dr. Finch leaned forward and tilted her head, and some tendrils of gray hair escaped from her bun. "I'm not going to lie. The trauma you've suffered is going to be with you for the rest of your life. Your job now, is to change your relationship with the trauma and learn to deal with it in a healthy way."

"So, if there's no cure, what is the point of treatment exactly?" Disappointment swept through Zaya, as she squeezed her hands together.

"We're going to work on honing your coping skills so that your life can be as normal as possible." Dr. Finch reached out and patted Zaya's arm. "You've lived through something that would have broken most people. That's amazing in itself. It tells me you've got the strength inside you to build a happy life."

Zaya took a breath and relaxed her hands. Her thumb grazed over the scars on her palms, the criss-crosses making an odd pattern, like a maze. Maybe that's what navigating her life would be like now. A strange maze. "Okay. What do I need to do?"

"Since you've only just returned, we're going to help you process what you've experienced. Watch for symptoms like flashbacks or nightmares or starting to feel detached, like you don't have a long-term future ahead of you. Whatever your needs are, that's what we'll work on." Dr. Finch shifted in her chair, so she was leaning on the arm toward Zaya. "A lot of times, the more you can talk about what happened to you, the less power the experience has. And if you can't say it out loud, keeping a journal and writing those things down can also be cathartic. Whatever feels most comfortable for you."

"I don't know if I could write any of it down," Zaya said. Fear crept down her spine at the thought of having her experience in black and white for anyone to read.

"That's okay. We can always just talk." Dr. Finch smiled and tucked a stray bit of hair behind her ear. "We don't even have to talk today. Whenever you feel like you need to get something out, I'll be here to listen."

Zaya looked over at the slightly plump and yet, compact, woman next to her. She seemed more like a grandmother who wouldn't be able to understand anything that Zaya had gone through. "I don't mean to be offensive, but I'm afraid if I tell you anything about my captivity, well, you'd be shocked enough to run from the room. You seem too . . . nice."

Dr. Finch chuckled. "Don't let my appearance fool you. I'm no delicate flower. I've been deployed to Iraq twice and have been in or around the military my entire life. My father and brothers were all in the army, so I joined, too, and met my husband. We had a wonderful life serving our country and seeing the world. I've never really known anything different until I settled here."

"Did your husband retire, then?" Zaya wasn't sure if she was supposed to be asking questions, but it was helping her get to know Dr. Finch better and feel more comfortable confiding in her.

Dr. Finch gave her a sad smile. "My husband came home from his tour in Iraq with severe PTSD. There weren't a lot of treatment options open for him, and what was available came across as a sort of one-size-fits-all approach. It wasn't working for him. He committed suicide." She closed her eyes briefly. "That's why I specialize in helping veterans with PTSD. My work helps me feel closer to him, in a way, by helping prevent similar outcomes for other veterans."

"I'm sorry." The words felt hollow, but Zaya wasn't sure what else to say. The woman had obviously suffered a great deal, more than Zaya had imagined. "I didn't mean to pry."

"It's okay. We all have experiences and trauma that shape us. The trick is finding a way to make peace with who we are and how we cope with the emotions." She looked at her watch. "It's nearly lunchtime. You need to keep up your strength, so let's stop here for today. I don't want to push you too hard on our very first visit."

"You haven't." Zaya ran her hands over her hair. "I can't seem to find my bearings, so I'm glad to have a little help." She ran her thumb over her palm scars again, Dr. Finch's words running through her mind that she was strong enough to do this. "There was one thing I wanted to ask."

Dr. Finch had started to rise, but sat back down. "What's that?"

Now that the moment was here, Zaya wasn't sure if she could say the words. It felt personal, maybe too private. She barely knew Dr. Finch. But she was a doctor and had suffered loss in her own life. *Just keep it general.*

"Both you and your husband were in the military. You saw and experienced difficult things, from different perspectives. How did you manage to connect with each other . . . after? Did you talk about what you'd experienced? Pretend it never happened?"

Dr. Finch looked thoughtful. "It depended on the situation, I guess. After his tour, my husband thought he was protecting me by not sharing how bad his nightmares were and how his flashbacks were getting more and more intense. With my job, there were a lot of things I couldn't tell him, but when I had the opportunity to share experiences, I did. I knew he'd understand, and when I spoke about things aloud, it helped me process." She shifted forward in her seat. "Are you worried you won't be able to connect with a husband or boyfriend?"

Julian's face flashed through Zaya's mind. His laughing eyes that weren't laughing anymore. Could they ever connect again after what they'd been through? "I had a boyfriend." Zaya lifted her chin and met Dr. Finch's gaze. "Commander Bennet, actually."

"I thought as much, but I try never to assume anything." She tapped her index finger on her chin. "Were you at the beginning of your relationship?"

She bit her lip. It might have been a little easier if they *had* just started to date. "Actually, we'd been talking about marriage. But now . . . everything is the opposite of what it used to be." Zaya gripped both armrests, wishing she could get up and pace, but with her injuries, she held herself still. "I can't relax. I'm always on edge. I mean, my head knows I'm safe, but I held a knife on Julian this morning, for pity's sake. How can I ever trust myself around him, or anyone for that matter?"

Dr. Finch didn't even raise an eyebrow, but her eyes seemed to see straight through to Zaya's innermost thoughts. "This probably isn't what you want to hear, but there aren't any easy answers. Both you and Commander Bennet will have to be patient as you find a new normal and learn where your relationship stands."

"Do you think we can get back what we had?" Zaya looked straight at Dr. Finch, though she wanted to close her eyes instead. She needed to see the doctor's face and gauge her body language when she answered. It was a skill that had come through for her when she'd dealt with Saif, and it might give her a clue to what Dr. Finch was truly thinking.

Her answer was everything.

Dr. Finch hesitated slightly, but smiled before she spoke. "Only the two of you can answer that, but, yes, I believe it's possible. I wouldn't close the door on anything just yet."

Zaya released a breath she hadn't realized she was holding. Relief washed over her. "Thanks."

Dr. Finch patted her arm. "Love can be very healing, but getting through the pain and guilt of what you've both suffered will test you. Just try to be as honest with each other as you can." She stood. "I'm going to go see about some lunch. We were told to keep your diet pretty bland for the first while, but you know what you can handle. Would you like some soup? A sandwich?"

"A sandwich sounds wonderful." Zaya's stomach grumbled in agreement, and both of the women laughed. "I don't need to be waited on hand and foot, though. I can come down with you."

Dr. Finch held up a hand. "No, you need to stay off of your feet. Let us help you, at least for these first few days." She walked toward the door, but stopped and turned. "Should I tell Commander Bennet we're finished and that he can come back in?"

Zaya's lips curved into a smile. "If he asks."

"I'd be surprised if he weren't right outside this door." She opened it, but Julian wasn't there.

Zaya laughed. "Believe me, he's always one to surprise people."

Dr. Finch chuckled. "I'll keep that in mind. Be right back with your lunch." Her no-nonsense shoes were silent on the stairs, but the words Dr. Finch had said during their session were loud in Zaya's mind. Patience had never been her strong suit, but figuring out her life from here on out was too important to rush. Having Dr. Finch to help did give her a boost of confidence, though. Maybe she was strong enough after all, and there could be a chance to find happiness with Julian.

She liked that thought. More than she should. She crossed her hands over her middle and smiled. Dr. Finch had said not to close any doors. That's where she would start. Cracking her heart open again would take courage, though, and that's where Zaya faltered. She'd survived Nazer and Saif, but she didn't know if she could recover from losing Julian.

She sighed, her momentary confidence fading. *Patience*, she told herself.

That was easy to tell herself, but harder to do. Slowly maneuvering her body, she stood and got back in bed. Pulling the covers over her shoulder, she closed her eyes, enjoying the feel of the sun streaming through the window. For right now, she was going to concentrate on the present and not worry about the future.

Light. Food. People who cared. She had everything and everyone she needed and even though she would eventually want more, in this moment, it was enough.

CHAPTER TWELVE

Julian strode toward the front door, adjusting his shoulder holster and gun as he walked. He yanked the door open, anxious to get on the road and find Elliott. Even the thought of another person he cared about being abducted by Nazer was enough to make bile rise in his throat.

"G-going somewhere?" Elliott was in the doorway, about to come in. "You're obviously in a big h-h-hurry. What's happened?" He walked into the house with a smile and it took a moment for Julian to speak. Elliott was here. He was fine.

"Where have you been? You haven't been answering your cell."

"I turned it off at the h-hospital and forgot to t-turn it back on." He raised guilty eyes to Julian. "I'm s-sorry. I know that's against p-protocol, but last night got p-pretty crazy at the h-hospital and I lent a hand."

"How's Charlie?" Julian asked, rolling his shoulders and giving his heart a second to return to normal. Elliott's stutter was worse when he was stressed and obviously, Julian's demeanor was making him anxious.

"B-better. They'll keep her for another d-day or so." Elliott glanced around. "You d-didn't say where you were g-going in such a hurry."

"I was coming to find you. With Nazer being spotted in England, we have to be on guard. You weren't accounted for." Julian folded his arms, remembering his fear for Elliott's safety. "We're upping security."

Elliott looked sheepish. "That's g-good to know. I'm s-sorry for being unreachable. How's Zaya?" He shifted his medical bag to his other hand. "Has her f-f-fever broken?"

"Last night. She did re-open her foot wound, though. I bandaged it as best I could, but I'd like you to take a look at it." He looked up as Dr. Finch came down the main stairs, her expression unreadable. Anxiety threaded through him. Their talk hadn't taken as long as he thought it would. "How did things go? Is everything all right?" he asked the older woman.

"Everything's fine. We got acquainted, and I'm going to get her some lunch." She passed the two men. "Would you two like something?"

"I ate not l-l-long ago," Elliott said. "Thanks, though."

"I was going to make cucumber sandwiches for Zaya's lunch," Julian said. "If you'll give me a minute, I'll take care of the food."

Dr. Finch held up a hand. "Let me. I like feeling useful, and I love cooking."

Well, he wouldn't say no to that, so Julian nodded. "Thanks. I appreciate all you've done for us, as well as for Zaya."

"That's what you pay me for." She grinned and started down the hall.

Elliott shook his head as they watched her go. "She's a character. Her r-r-reputation for helping veterans is unsurpassed, though. I'm really surprised you got her to take a leave of absence from her practice."

"It's only for a few weeks. Zaya needed the best available to her." He'd wanted Zaya to have everything he could possibly provide to make her recovery smoother. "I hoped she'd be safe enough here to heal, but with Nazer coming for her, that won't happen." He stopped at the bottom of the stairs. "We've got to get eyes on this guy and make sure he's far away from Zaya."

Elliott put his hand on Julian's arm. "W-we will. You've t-trained us all for this, so trust that and don't worry." He passed Julian and started upstairs. "Now let me go see my p-patient."

They resumed their climb, but were only halfway up the stairs when Augie called out. "I've got that laptop you wanted, boss." He held out the computer.

"Why don't you come and give it to her? Then you can update her on what you've already found in your research." Julian once again turned back toward the stairs, belatedly realizing Zaya could be emotional from her meeting with Dr. Finch. Maybe he should go in before Elliott or Augie, just to make sure she was okay. But Elliott was already ahead of him and knocked briefly before entering. Julian and Augie weren't far behind.

She was curled up in bed, her eyes sleepy as they entered. Her smile was slow in coming, but got bigger as she eyed each one of them. "What's going on?"

Julian stepped forward, taking off his shoulder holster and setting it on the nightstand. "Elliott wanted to look at your foot, and Augie brought the laptop so you can start researching. But we can come back later," he hastily added.

Her eyes showed a flicker of excitement, but her yawn showed how tired she really was. "Sounds good. I'm sorry. I'm just so tired. Can you let Dr. Finch know I'll eat something later?"

"That's not a problem. The food will be ready when you wake up." Julian turned to Elliott and Augie. "Can you go down and let her know?"

Augie nodded, a chunk of his red hair flopping over his brow before he pushed it back. "I will," he said, before he left.

Elliott stood next to Julian. "Do you think the rebandaging job you did will hold for a couple of hours?"

Julian frowned. "I do have basic medical skills, you know."

Elliott gave a low laugh. "All right. I'll wait to check on it then." He moved toward the door, but turned when Julian didn't follow. "You coming?"

"In a minute." He was torn, wanting to stay here with Zaya, but not wanting to make her feel smothered.

"I'll just shut the door," Elliott said, closing it softly after him.

Julian moved toward the chair, scooting it closer to the bed as quietly as he could. Zaya looked like she was asleep already, but when he sat down, she reached out for him. He held her hand in his, her small fingers so delicate and white against his larger tanned ones. His thumb stroked the back of her hand, and he turned it toward him so he could see the criss-cross scars that lashed her palm. He could only imagine the pain she'd felt with every strike and he couldn't catch his breath. Guilt swamped him. In the back of her mind, would she always blame him?

He looked at her sleeping face, and reached out to touch her cheek. She'd held on, waited for him to come for her. She was a survivor, and he would spend the rest of his life making sure she didn't regret coming out of that prison alive.

Zaya slept until dinnertime. When she woke up, she ate two sandwiches, a bowl of soup, and some pudding. She seemed less fragile and more anxious to engage with the team, so Julian brought her downstairs to the sitting room where a TV had been set up. Augie was there with his laptop, trying to put together an untraceable connection for a movie to stream on. Julian busied himself getting a fire going in the fireplace.

"This is cozy," she said, tucking the afghan around her legs. "Did you tell everyone we were starting the movie soon?"

"I think they're waiting on Nate." Julian used the poker to push a log closer to the flame.

"Accounted for," Nate said, as he came in. He crossed the room to Zaya and reached out a hand. "Nice to finally meet you when we aren't under fire."

She took his hand with a chuckle. "I agree. Thanks for coming to get me." She shifted a bit. "I was starting to wonder if you'd come to the house with the rest of the team."

"I've been running perimeter security." He turned to Julian. "I shifted some cameras around and made sure the edge of the property is in range. Elliott's finishing up a call with Charlie, then he'll join us."

"Something wrong with Charlie's recovery?" Julian asked, as he joined Zaya on the couch.

"No. Sounded like a social call to me." He took the chair next to them. "Did we decide on a movie?"

Brenna came in with a big bowl of popcorn, Colt not far behind her. "All we had to choose from were *The Princess Bride* or *Ferris Bueller's Day Off.*" She shot an accusing look at Augie.

He didn't even blink. "When you're staying off the grid, you have to take what you can get."

"I love *The Princess Bride*," Zaya said, reaching for some popcorn. "I haven't seen it in ages."

When Mya came in, Augie jumped up, hurrying to help her balance the drinks. Once they were passed out, and everyone in their seats, Elliott joined them, carrying his medical supplies.

"Sorry I'm late. Do we have time for a quick wound check?"

Zaya smiled. "Maybe. If you tell us how things are going with Charlie."

Elliott flushed. "W-what do you mean? She's f-fine."

"We heard you were chatting with her." Zaya teased. "Is it too cliché for a doctor to fall in love with his nurse?"

"We're j-just talking," Elliott mumbled, standing next to Zaya's couch.

"All right, all right, we'll let you have your privacy," Julian said, chuckling. He'd never seen Elliott this flustered before. Charlie must be someone pretty important to be eliciting this sort of reaction.

"But we haven't gotten any dirt," Brenna protested.

"There isn't any d-dirt," Elliott said as he knelt down and shot Brenna a wicked grin. "Yet."

"Ohhh," Zaya said as she swung her legs out from under the afghan and stuck out her foot to Elliott. "Will you tell us when there is?"

"No. You'll j-just have to wonder." He started to unwrap the bandage. "Doesn't look like Julian's wrap job turned out too badly. Has your fever come back?" Elliott asked.

"No." She glanced at Julian. "I felt like I was on fire last night, but today's been a lot better."

Julian remembered the things her fevered brain had let slip. Would she ever feel comfortable confiding them when she was lucid? "Well, better until you decided to go for a walk on an infected foot."

"Are you tattling on me?" she asked, with a quirk of her eyebrows.

"Yes," he said with a grin. "If Elliott's wrath will keep you off your foot, I'm all for tattling."

Elliott didn't respond, just removed the bandage to examine her wound. "It doesn't look too bad," he said finally. "The antibiotics are doing their job. The best thing we can do now is keep off it." He started to rebandage it. "I brought along some crutches, so that will help your mobility."

"Which may or may not be a good thing," Julian joked, and Zaya playfully glared at him.

Augie set down his laptop and brought a case over to her. "Here's your laptop for when you feel up to doing some research." He chewed his thumbnail, a telltale sign that he was anxious. "I could show you what I've done already and where I could use your help. It will just take a minute, and then you'll be ready to go tomorrow."

"That would be great." She patted the seat next to her. "I appreciate everything you've done for me, and I hope I can repay the favor."

Augie smiled and sat down, taking the laptop out of the case and opening it. In no time at all, it was booted up and ready to go. "I've done spreadsheets and kept records of all Nazer's shell companies, payouts to individuals, and banks he's used. That's here." He pointed to a file. "Then I broke that down to transaction numbers, account numbers we know, that sort of thing."

Zaya leaned over to look. "That's a big file."

"Hopefully it all makes sense, or will after you've had a chance to look at it." He pointed to another file. "This is all the information I've gathered so far on Nazer's child. And the boy's mother."

"That's where I come in?" Zaya looked up at Julian.

"Yes. The more we know on that situation, the easier it will be to predict Nazer's next move. If we can just get more than a step ahead of him, I think we have a chance of capturing him." Julian nodded to Augie. "Your and Augie's research is key."

Zaya looked down at Elliott, who was just finishing up with her foot. "We can start first thing in the morning."

"Just remember not to overtax y-yourself. You need rest, too." Elliott patted her knee and stood. He glanced over at Julian. "Don't let her do t-too much."

"I'll do my best." Julian gave her a speaking glance. "It won't be easy, though."

Zaya didn't even look up as she closed the laptop. "You two would have made terrible nannies."

"You w-wound me," Elliott said, his hand next to his heart. "I would have m-made an exceptional n-nanny. Kids love me, and I can bandage all their boo-boos and kiss the hurt away."

The Capture

Julian bent low and looked into Zaya's face. "If kissing your boo-boo will change your bad opinion of me, I'm willing to make the sacrifice." He heard her breath hitch and gave her a half-smile. "I'm happy to kiss anywhere that hurts."

Her body went perfectly still as he reached for her hands, her brown eyes darkening to nearly black, but at the last moment, she pulled away before he could touch her. "I'm fine, thanks." She turned away, flustered enough that she banged her hand against the laptop. "Is the movie ready?"

Julian turned away so she wouldn't see his smile. He hadn't imagined her reaction. Their connection was very much alive, he knew that much. It just needed some tender-loving care to keep that tiny flicker burning.

The next two hours were filled with lots of popcorn and laughter as they watched the show and quoted all the funny lines. Near the end, Zaya's head was drooping toward Julian's shoulder, so he moved closer, and she let it fall, snuggling close. For just a moment, all those months of suffering vanished, and it was just them in the here and now. He breathed in the scent of her shampoo and wished reality wouldn't crash in on them so soon. But the credits were rolling, and he knew they only had a few more minutes like this before she'd go to bed and probably have to face the nightmares.

"That was really fun," Brenna said as she started gathering the popcorn bowls. "I'd forgotten how much I like that show."

"Me, too," Zaya said, covering her yawn. "I'm glad I was able to stay mostly awake through the whole thing." She sat up straighter and Julian shifted away from her a little bit, though he stayed close. "I don't know if I've ever been this tired, though."

"Your b-body is still fighting off the infection. You should d-definitely listen to it and get some extra rest," Elliot supplied. "Which is a b-big hint to head to bed."

Julian stood and she looked up at him. "Could you carry me? I'm a little dizzy."

Julian's eyes cut over to Elliott, and he held up his hand. "Dizziness is normal, boss."

"Okay." His heart skipped a beat as he bent to pick her up. "I'm always happy to help a damsel in distress."

"Never mind," Zaya said, as she tried to stand on her own. "I can't do the damsel thing."

"I was kidding." He took her arm and placed it around his neck. "I know you better than anyone else. There's not an ounce of distressed damsel in you."

"Don't you forget it," she said with a hmmph. Everyone laughed, and once she was in his arms, they all wished her a good night with smiles on their faces.

Julian climbed the stairs and, while they didn't say much on the way up to her room, the silence was comfortable. When he sat her on the bed, she slid her hand down the stubble on his cheek. "Thank you."

He kissed her forehead. "Anytime. I'm next door, so if you need anything tonight, I can be here in ten seconds flat."

"Should I time you?" she asked, with a tired smile.

"Only if you don't trust me." He smoothed the covers around her, wishing he dared take her in his arms and stay with her again tonight. When she didn't respond, his last words sank into his brain. "Wait, that didn't come out—"

She put her fingers on his lips. "I know what you meant. Let's just take it one day at a time, okay?"

He leaned down and tucked a piece of hair behind her ear. "Sounds like a great plan."

She quirked up a corner of her mouth. "Of course it is. I thought of it."

"Touché." He laughed and let his hand slide down her arm. This was how it had been between them before, easy and comfortable. "I missed you."

Her eyes clouded for just a minute, but the shadow disappeared as quickly as it came. "I know. But, Julian . . ."

Julian took a step back. "I know, I know. It's complicated." He couldn't stall any longer. "Night." He turned on the lamp next to the bed. "If you decide you want it dark, the switch is here." He pointed to the bottom of the lamp. She nodded, and her eyes were already closing so he left the room with one last glance at her.

For a day that had started out so badly, it had ended so much better than he could have imagined.

CHAPTER THIRTEEN

The first two nights after the movie were filled with nightmares so real that Zaya woke up in a blind panic, soaked in sweat. Julian was always by her side in an instant, and Dr. Finch soon joined him. At first, Zaya had been embarrassed, but it quickly turned to gratitude. Dr. Finch seemed to know exactly what she needed to help her through. Mindful breathing had helped a lot, combined with meditation and relaxation techniques, but the one thing she thought she'd never do—journal writing—was what had made the most impact.

She sat on a wooden bench on the sunny side of the property, her pen poised in the air as she thought about what she wanted to write next.

"How's the image rehearsal therapy coming?" Julian asked, as he sat down next to her.

"Better. Writing a positive outcome is harder than it seems, though. I can write my dreams in detail. Saif or Nazer is always there, waiting to recapture me and throw me in that prison again. The darkness is following me, waiting for me, no matter how far or fast I run. But actually writing a better ending is hard." She put the pen in the middle of the pages and shut the book. "So far I've just made sure Nazer can never touch me, and I'm able to run from the darkness."

"Sounds like a good start." He leaned back and slid his arm across her shoulders. "Were you able to fall back asleep last night?"

"No. I went ahead and worked on some research for Augie. There's enough work in tracking Nazer for five computer techs." She couldn't help herself; she took in an extra big breath to smell Julian's aftershave. How could anyone smell so good? "Dr. Finch is pretty amazing, though. I'm not as afraid as before to try to sleep."

"Maybe you can catch a nap this afternoon." He played with the end of her hair just below her ear. "It seems like you're able to sleep better when it's light."

She was always surprised when he noticed so many details about her. It made her feel cherished. "I like the routine we're starting, though. Even without a full night's sleep, I like having breakfast with the team, then working for Augie while you run everyone through some drills. A little bit of normal to look forward to."

"The drills are good to keep our skills sharp," Julian said, "but waiting for Nazer to make a move is taking a toll on all of us."

"Maybe you should try mindful breathing to take your mind off of it." She leaned into his shoulder and just took in the house and grounds. "It's so beautiful here. When I come out early in the morning to watch the sunrise, I'm grateful for so many things: the wind on my face, the smell of trees and flowers, the sun and sky. It's weird how being in prison made those things so precious."

He squeezed her shoulders and kissed the top of her head. "I'm glad you're here."

They both looked over the landscape, just enjoying being together. There weren't many flowers left, but the grounds were still pretty and mostly green.

Zaya was the first to break the silence. "You know, we've been concentrating so much on my recovery, I think maybe you have some things bottled up that need to be said. Out loud." She sat up a little straighter, knowing that this might be a hard conversation to have.

"Like what?" He drew back as if he was going to let go of her hand, but she put her other hand over his so he couldn't.

"Like, why do you apologize to me so often?" she asked. "You don't have anything to be sorry about." She tilted her head, surprised at how anxious he looked. "What are you really thinking about?"

"I know you blame me for your abduction, and I take responsibility for that. It was my fault. I just wish there was something more I could do to help you now." He turned away from her. "It kills me to see you hurting."

She pressed her lips together. "I thought as much." Taking his chin in her hand, she turned his face toward her, letting her thumb settle in the cleft of his chin. "I want you to hear me when I say this."

"You don't have to say anything," he said, putting his hand over hers and letting them fall to his lap.

She shook her head and twisted on the bench to look in his eyes. "I *don't* blame you for my abduction, and you're not responsible for any of it. All the blame belongs on Nazer's shoulders." Moving closer, she put her hands on his biceps and drew him into her space. "And you *are* helping me. Every day. Just you being here helps me, makes me feel safe."

He took her in, letting his eyes roam over her face. She hoped he could see how sincere she was in her words.

"Z," he whispered before he crushed her to him, like a man grasping a life preserver, murmuring more words into her hair that she couldn't make out.

She smiled, his relief and happiness chasing away more of the uncertainty that had been between them. She hugged him back, holding him tight against her. "You know, Nate probably has security cameras trained on us right now."

A low laugh rumbled through his chest under her ear. "I don't care," he said, but he drew back, tucking her under his arm. "We'll just make him jealous."

"Have you heard any more about Elliott and Charlie?" She snuggled closer, enjoying his warm body next to hers.

"Jake says he's been talking to Charlie every night." Julian made lazy circles on her arm. "We may need to make room on the team for a nurse."

"Would you do that?" She pulled back to look at him. Before, he only hired Griffin Force members who had essential skills. Their private lives never came into the equation. This was definitely a departure for him.

"I know what you're thinking, but after your abduction, a lot of things came into focus for me. To tell the truth, once we capture Nazer, I'm thinking about turning Griffin Force over to Colt. He's got the aptitude for it and can take it to the next level." He pushed her hair back from her cheek. "What do you think?"

Zaya raised her eyebrows. "You would really give up Griffin Force? It's been your life for so long."

"Maybe that's not my life anymore." His knuckles gently grazed her cheek. "I don't want to be chasing criminals or looking over my shoulder my entire life. I want to settle down, get married, and have a family."

His touch and the words coming out of his mouth were sending a swarm of butterflies flapping in her middle. He was everything she'd ever wanted, and Dr. Finch had given her hope that she could still lead a normal life. Could she be part of the future Julian was talking about?

"Julian . . ." she started, but stopped when Augie's voice called for her nearby.

"The guy has terrible timing," Julian complained, but he moved back to put a little more space between them. He didn't let go of her hand, though, and she was glad.

Augie came into view a few seconds later. "There you are. I thought we were going to dig into that new file we found this morning."

Zaya nodded, her mouth curving into a smile as she watched Julian scowl. "I'll be right in."

"Do you need your crutches?" Augie asked, looking around for them.

"I'm walking on my own today," Zaya said proudly. It was probably a little too soon, but her foot felt so much better, and she wanted to be free of the crutches.

"Do you think that's a good idea?" Julian asked with concern.

"Yes," she said, bumping his shoulder. "I'm fine." Standing, she followed Augie back into the house, with Julian bringing up the rear. Augie kept up a one-sided conversation that only required a nod or shake of the head occasionally. He was brilliant with a computer, but at times, it seemed he'd forgotten that human conversation had two sides.

"Do you mind if I go get my laptop? I left it in my room." Zaya started for the stairs, but Julian put a hand on her arm.

"Why don't we work from your room today, so you can rest if you need to?" He looked more worried than he should, so she agreed, hoping to erase that look from his face completely.

"Okay. Are you going to work with us today, too?" She turned and started up the steps, knowing it would take her an extra minute to climb them. Her foot was better, but stairs were still difficult.

"If you don't mind." He stayed next to her, ready to offer support if she needed it, but giving her enough space to do it on her own. Her heart fluttered a little more at his understanding of her need for independence. He really was the perfect man for her.

"I don't mind." She smiled and looked back at Augie. "Do you?"

"No," he said, following them close behind. "But we won't have a lot of time for conversation."

Julian raised his hands in mock surrender. "Okay, mate, I get the hint."

Once they made it to her room and settled in at the sitting area, the next hour was filled with the tapping of keys with a short break for lunch. Augie and Zaya didn't speak much, but looked over the other's shoulder occasionally. Julian figured out some contingency plans in the event Nazer tried to breach the house, when Zaya shifted her laptop over to Augie.

"Look at this."

Both Augie and Julian looked over at her screen where she was pointing.

"We know the payments for the child started about two years ago at 50,000 pounds a month," she said. "That's a lot of money to support a child, right?"

"Maybe he's trying to make up for lost time," Augie put in.

Zaya nodded and turned back to the screen. "That's probably when he found out he had a son, but look at this. Almost 40,000 was withdrawn in cash from the same account, within an hour or two of the deposit. Where did that money go? The mother has no assets to speak of, she lives in a middle-class neighborhood, doesn't employ a nanny, and has a job. Her financials don't reveal much of a savings or any offshore accounts." She sat back and tapped her chin while staring at the screen. "She has a Child Investment Plan to save for college."

Julian crossed his arms over his chest. "So, you're saying that Nazer uses his child to launder money and finance his terrorist network?" He shook his head at the thought. Even for a terrorist, that seemed like a new low.

"Forty thousand pounds a month, withdrawn every month, over a two year period, equals about 1.2 million U.S. dollars. Yet there's no sign of that kind of money on the mother's end." Zaya looked over at Augie. "Can we track it somehow?"

Augie bit his thumbnail. "Let me run a few programs and see what I can come up with." He typed furiously for a moment, then sat back. "What was the name of the investment firm she uses for the Child Plan?"

"Sharman Levin Financial Group." This time Zaya was the one looking over Augie's shoulder. "Why?"

He didn't answer right away, just tapped a few more keys. When he looked up at Julian, his eyes were wide. "Because Amelia Sinclair, the wife of William Sinclair, is on the board of directors. What if Nazer is using Caroline and Amelia to funnel the funds?"

Julian's breath caught in his throat at the suggestion. "William's wife?" The implication sank into his heart. He'd met Amelia on a few occasions. She was headstrong and opinionated, but loved her husband. Would there be any reason she would accept money from Nazer? Was she in on it with William? "Do we have any evidence at all the money went to the investment group or to Amelia?"

"Give me a minute." Augie started clicking through some files, but Julian hardly heard him, his brain trying to fathom the possibility that William could be the leak. What if Nazer was blackmailing William because of something Amelia had done? Could William be the reason Nazer always stayed one step ahead of him?

Augie got up from the end of the bed and reached for his laptop. He looked at Zaya apologetically. "I need some of my files from downstairs. Maybe you can help me search once I get them organized."

Zaya smiled. "No problem. You know where to find me."

Augie left and Julian leaned back in his chair, his mind still spinning. "William." He could barely say his name past the lump in his throat.

Zaya reached out and touched his shoulder. "We don't know anything for sure yet."

Julian got up and started pacing. "Of course he's involved. We found a connection to Nazer that William has never mentioned. We know that someone in intelligence is feeding Nazer information. Only a handful of people knew about Camp Bastion and you. Who else could the mole be?" He finally stopped pacing and folded his arms, staring down at her. "He's been to the safehouse. What if he's told Nazer where you are?"

A chill of foreboding went through her, but Julian was so worried that she tried to reassure him. "If William was the mole, something would have happened by now."

"He was my mentor, the person who made me feel like I could do this." Julian made another turn on his pacing route. "I don't have another explanation, but I don't want it to be true."

"Don't jump to conclusions." As she said the words, the hairs on the back of her neck stood up. Immediately looking around, she spotted a small red laser searching for a target through the window. "Shooter! Get down!" She grabbed Julian and pulled him to the floor with her.

Taking cover on the far side of the bed, Julian scrambled to keep her out of harm's way. "Stay right here and keep your head down. I'm going to see if I can get a look."

She nodded, but her stomach was in knots as he belly crawled to the side of the window. Should she call out for the team downstairs? Her throat seemed paralyzed, so she put her hands over her head, instead.

Please don't let him die, she chanted over and over in her mind.

And then the window shattered.

CHAPTER FOURTEEN

Glass shards dug into Julian's skin from the broken window, but at least no other shots came. He levered himself up and peeked out, but nothing was moving outside. Was that a warning shot? So many tactical thoughts ran through his mind, but one crowded those out.

Zaya.

He dropped back to his knees and crawled to where he'd left her. "Z, you okay?"

"Yeah," she said, but her voice came out in a sob, and when she looked at him, she was pale, her eyes wide. "Your cheek's bleeding. Were you grazed?"

He touched his hand to his face and looked at the blood on his fingers. "I think it was just glass from the window." He gave her a visual once-over. "Are you sure you're not hurt?"

"I'm fine."

Julian couldn't see any visible injuries, but an event like this would have repercussions on her already overtaxed emotions. He clenched his jaw, shoving down the urge to punch the wall at the unfairness of it all. "I don't want to leave you alone, but I have to see what's going on. Will you be all right for a minute?"

She nodded, but her eyes looked unsure. Julian's gut twisted. She should be enjoying her freedom and recovering from her ordeal, not dodging bullets again. "I know you want to come down with me, but I think it's better if you're up here until I know what's going on. I won't be long." He leaned closer, pressing his forehead to hers. "I'm sorry, Z. No matter what I do, I can't seem to keep you safe."

"It's not you." She reached up and cupped his cheek. "This isn't your fault. This is on the mole, whether it's William or Nazer. We've got to stop them." She trembled, but all Julian could think of was her sweet voice saying it wasn't his fault. The more she said it, the more his heart wanted to believe her.

He took her fingers in his own. "I'll lock the door behind me. Don't let anyone in."

She held onto his hand so tight he nearly winced. "Promise me you'll be careful."

His heart broke a little bit at the desperation in her tone, but he squeezed her fingers in reassurance before he pulled away. "I promise." Her eyes were bright with unshed tears, and he lightly touched her chin. "Don't worry. You won't get rid of me that easily."

She gave him a small smile, and it took everything he had to get up and leave her. He locked the door behind him.

Jogging down the stairs, he met Brenna on the way up, her gun drawn.

"Glad to see you're okay," she said, letting her hand drop to her side. "How's Zaya?"

"Physically, she's fine." He followed her down the stairs and they headed for the back entryway to the small room set up for communications. "She saw the laser targeting a millisecond before the shot and warned me." He still marveled at how good her instincts were after all these months.

They entered the room and went immediately to the security monitors, finding the one that would give them the best view of the area where the shot had originated.

"We got the shooter," she told him, pointing to the corner of the surveillance screen. "But he's dead. Jake says the guy isn't Nazer or anyone we know from his organization."

Julian stifled a frustrated groan. It would have been nice to take him alive so they could question him. At least this guy wouldn't be coming after them again, but Nazer had plenty of other men he could use. So did William. "What happened?"

"Jake thought he saw something in the far corner of the property, so he went out to investigate. Saw the guy a second too late." Brenna's gaze went back to the screen. "Colt was on the other side of the house when he heard the shot, and immediately went over for backup."

Julian could read her worried look about Colt being out there, but knew she'd never admit to it. Colt was one of the best operatives he'd seen in the field and could handle himself. While that was comforting, it was still tough to see the person you love in harm's way.

"We're going to have to call a higher-up in on this. I don't want the local constabulary mucking about on the property, asking a lot of questions we can't answer." He stepped closer to the monitor, watching the trees where Colt and Jake were now bending over the body. Normally, he would have called William about an incident like this, but that wasn't an option. Yet, at the same time, maybe it was. The seeds of a plan to draw William into a confession started to form. What if he called William here, and asked him some pointed questions, something that could trip him up and show his guilt?

Brenna touched his arm, bringing him back to the present. "How's Zaya handling all this? As if she didn't already have enough to deal with."

"About as you would expect." Julian leaned his hip against the desk, thinking of the fear in Zaya's face. William had been trusted with so much information about Zaya, her rescue, the plans for her safety. If he truly was working with a terrorist, and Julian let him near the house, he would be giving Nazer direct access to Zaya all over again. The knowledge lodged in his gut. He had to confront William without tipping his hand. Not until they had iron-clad proof, enough to put him away for life. "I need to get back to her, but I'll call William first."

Protocol demanded that William take Zaya into protective custody, which was probably William's plan all along if he were working with Nazer. It would be easier for them to eliminate her, if she was in their custody. He needed to get Zaya out of here and figure out a way to keep her safe that didn't include William.

"Do you want to use the phone in here?" Brenna pointed to the one on the desk. "I can check to see if Colt or Jake need anything."

"No, I'll go to the library. Keep monitoring them from here, just in case the shooter wasn't alone." With one last look at the man down, Julian walked into the library. His mind was racing as he ran through some quick scenarios of how to deal with William. One thing was certain; he had to see the man he'd respected and confided in face to face. He dialed his direct line, and William picked up on the second ring.

William didn't bother with a greeting. "Surprised to hear from you after our conversation a couple of days ago, Commander."

"We've had a little problem out here," Julian said. "I need your help handling it." His words were measured and confident. Nothing would seem out of the ordinary.

"I'll be right there." And with that, he hung up.

Julian stared at the phone in his hand a moment. He didn't know what he'd been expecting from William, but it wasn't that. Shoving the phone back onto the desk, he let out a long breath. Even though he'd been running Griffin Force on his own for a few years, it had always been comforting to be able to count on William as a backup and mentor. All of that was gone now, though. His fists clenched.

The Capture

Why? Why would William help Nazer in any way? After all the attacks, murder, kidnappings, torture, Nazer deserved to be hunted and locked up. Julian had thought William understood and believed the same thing. Never once had he ever suspected William could sympathize with a terrorist.

He unclenched his fists and rolled his neck before he left the library and walked back to Brenna in the communications room. He'd have to bring the rest of the team in on this sooner or later, but he'd wait until they were all together.

"Have we secured the perimeter?" he asked, when he entered the comm room.

"All clear. We didn't find a vehicle yet, or any indication of how the shooter got onto the property." Brenna sat on the chair in front of the monitors. "Since we didn't get a hit on the shooter's fingerprints, Augie is working on facial recognition."

"Okay. Let me know if anything comes up. William is on his way." Julian folded his arms. He needed to talk to Zaya and bring her up to speed. Maybe she would have some ideas on how to best deal with William until positive proof came through. "I'm going to go check on Zaya."

He headed back upstairs, trying to figure out how to tell Zaya what he'd decided to do about William. He knocked softly on her door. "Z, it's me."

No answer. Alarm swept over him as he unlocked the door with the key.

Zaya wasn't anywhere to be seen.

He went to the window, but could only see shadows moving through the trees as Colt and Jake kept watch over the body. Julian checked the bathroom and under the bed. Nothing. Where could she be?

I shouldn't have left her, his mind screamed. But then he heard it. A small muffled sound coming from the closet. He strode over and slowly opened the door. Zaya was huddled in the corner. "Z. Sweetheart."

She was curled in a ball, with her hands over her head. He crouched down and softly touched her shoulder. "Z, it's me. Julian."

She lifted her gaze, eyes swimming with tears, and held out her arms to him. He didn't think twice. He folded her into his embrace as she sobbed quietly. He rubbed his hands over her back. She was so cold, he wanted to warm her with his body heat, and make her demons go away by sheer force of will. They stayed like that, half-in and half-out of the closet, until her sobs subsided. She lay quietly against his chest, and he stroked her hair.

"I'm here," he murmured. "I'll never leave you again."

Her fist curled into his shirtfront. "I couldn't bear it if anything happened to you," she said, her voice hoarse from tears. "Even with things so unsettled between us, I need you alive."

He pressed her closer. "I'm not planning on dying anytime soon."

She lifted her head to look him in the face. "Did you find whoever's shooting at us? Was it Nazer?"

"No, but it was probably someone associated with him." He didn't mention William's name. Even though he'd decided to be honest with her, he briefly thought about shielding her from what was happening. He quickly discarded that idea, though. She needed to know. "Z, I've confided a lot of our plans to William so I would have every base covered when we got you back. Now that we know he has a connection to Nazer, though, we need to make new plans."

"What are you thinking?" Her voice trembled, and Julian second-guessed himself one more time. She needed to feel secure and safe, neither of which he was providing at the moment.

"I want to draw William out somehow, but when we do that, I want you in an undisclosed location. Somewhere only you and I know." He touched her hair. "He's on his way here now, so we're going to have to move quickly. I'm sorry."

"Julian, this isn't making sense to me. If William is the backer, why hasn't he given you up to Nazer by now? Why would he kidnap me to get answers about you, when William knows everything about Griffin Force? Something doesn't add up." She drummed her fingers against his chest. "What if we let him debrief me and try to catch him in a lie? If he's truly a traitor, he'll know details of my captivity that no one else but me would know."

Julian hesitated, all the ways that scenario could go wrong and Zaya could end up hurt immediately flooding his mind. "I don't know. That would be pretty risky, and even if he did know a few details, that wouldn't be proof necessarily."

"It'll give you some direction. If he has the information, or you think he's lying during the debrief, then he's the backer. If not, he might not have betrayed you. Either way, you'll have some idea about what to do next." Her voice sounded stronger and as she talked, Julian wanted to pump his fist in victory. The hope they could really come back from all that had happened and find a new, yet sort of familiar normal, was growing by the second.

"Are you sure?" He rested his cheek on the top of her head, rubbing her back with lazy circles like he'd always done before. If only they could stay like this for longer.

"Yes." Her eyes were bright with plans before she laid her cheek right over his heart. "I want to know where William stands as badly as you do. Just let me get cleaned up and we can go down together to wait for him."

He pulled back enough so she could see his smile and cradled her face in his hands. "You and I are a good team. Always have been."

A corner of her mouth lifted. "You know what? We're a brilliant team. Let's get that right."

And for that small moment, sitting on the floor of a dark closet, Julian's heart burned with the promise of a possible future with Zaya.

173

CHAPTER FIFTEEN

Zaya's palms were sweating, and instead of eating the scone in front of her, she was more or less just breaking it into small pieces on her plate. After hiding in the closet, fear coursing through her, the thought of letting William ask her questions to try and trap him into revealing he was Nazer's backer overwhelmed her, even though it was her idea. She didn't want Julian to hear her debrief, but at the same time she wanted him there to hold her hand. He was sitting beside her, his attention on the window and what was happening with the gunman's body at the edge of the wood not far from the house.

"You should go out there and get an update before William arrives. I'm fine." Zaya tore another piece of scone into crumbs. Sometimes it felt like that's all that was left of her life. Crumbs.

Julian's hand covered hers. "I'm afraid if I do, the scones won't forgive me."

She smiled and put her hands in her lap. "Too obvious?"

"It's okay to be nervous." He squeezed her fingers. "I'll be right here."

"That's part of what's bothering me." She turned in her chair. "The debrief is going to be hard. Living through it again . . ." Could he understand? She met his eyes, hoping she wouldn't have to spell it out. He'd always had a sixth sense when it came to her feelings, and had shown that ability at times since her rescue, but had that changed?

"You think it'll be too hard for me?" He let out a breath. "I can handle it, Z. And the moment he reveals himself, we can stop."

"The thing is, I don't want your pity or feeling any guilt." It was good to get that out, to have him know.

He let go of her fingers and raked a hand through his hair. "I've never pitied you. Even knowing a small part of what you went through tells me you're the strongest woman I know. And I'm struggling with the guilt still, but I'm working on it."

"I know." She wanted to reach for him again, to reassure him, but changed her mind when she heard footsteps in the hall.

The kitchen door opened, and Brenna stuck her head in. "Chief Sinclair is here. Are you sure you wouldn't be more comfortable meeting with him in the library instead of the kitchen? It's a little warmer in there."

William pushed his way around her. "Thanks for your concern, but really, the kitchen works for me. Especially if there's food." He sat down at the table and sniffed. "Something smells good."

Zaya nodded toward the small plate of scones in the middle of the table. "Help yourself."

"Zaya," William said, as he met her eyes for the first time. "I'm so glad to see you home safe and sound." He took a scone, but didn't take a bite. "We were all so worried about you."

Were you really? Zaya wanted to say, but the words clogged her throat. She had to keep it together, try to trap him. "I'm just glad to be home." She lifted her chin. "There were so many times I never thought I'd see England again."

"I heard Julian found you in Afghanistan. Do you remember any of the other countries you were held in?" He busied himself with putting jam on his scone and didn't meet her eyes when he asked the question.

"I was drugged a lot of the time, so I'm not really sure. There were several houses, one tent, and the prison you found me in." She looked over at Julian. "Did you give Chief Sinclair regular updates on your search?"

"I only shared actionable intel with William. So, while I wouldn't call them regular updates, he did get updates." As Julian spoke, Zaya could see the tension around his eyes, and she hoped William didn't look too close or think it had anything to do with him. He couldn't be suspicious at all, or this wouldn't work.

"MI6 did some searching as well," William said before he took a bite of his scone. "You were one of ours once, too, you know."

She remembered. It had been a happy time, overall, but moving on to Griffin Force had been the next step up the career ladder, and she'd taken it without hesitation. "I appreciate that. Did any of your investigations show how Nazer knew so many details about our convoy in Morocco? Someone on the inside had to give him details of the pickup and route to the airport. Those things were classified, right?"

William swallowed and brushed some crumbs off his shirt. "Probably the same mole Julian thinks is backing Nazer and leaking information. We know it's someone in intelligence, but we haven't narrowed it further."

"Augie's been doing some digging and found some interesting details," Julian started, but Zaya gave him a pointed look. They didn't want to tip their hand. Not yet. Julian continued anyway. "And we're pretty sure it's someone at MI6."

William immediately started to shake his head. "That's impossible. You know the stringent background checks our officers are required to have to even step through headquarter doors. We keep everyone on a tight leash." William put his scone down. "Do you have a name?"

"We're close." Julian leaned back, looking casual, as if he weren't trying to get a reaction from someone they'd long admired and respected. "Maybe you should narrow down your internal investigation to your office."

"I trust everyone in my office implicitly." William's voice had gone quiet. "If you're hinting at something, just say it. Are you making an accusation against someone?"

"No, but the moment I have concrete proof, I'll let you know," Julian assured him. "For now, I'd like to keep the details of our investigation to myself."

"That's not going to work with me. If my unit has been compromised, I need to know. What evidence could you possibly have that would point to my office?" William asked, his brows furrowed into a deep frown. He turned to Zaya. "Do you know what he's got?"

She shifted in her seat. "Julian will bring you in the moment he can. I'm sure you understand the need to be extra careful." The tension in the room ratcheted up a notch. William was not taking this well. Was that a sign of guilt?

"My office is being accused of having a traitor. I want to know what you have *now*." His voice was raised now, and his face was turning red.

"You're not the commanding officer here," Julian reminded him. "We have a courtesy relationship, that's all."

"Courtesy? I thought there was friendship and respect between us." William leaned over the table, his hands clasped in front of him. "Julian, we're talking about such a small circle of people, and I'd trust all of them with my life. I can't imagine even a shred of evidence against any of them panning out."

"That's why you need to look closer." Julian shook his head. "Especially at the smallest details that Nazer could exploit."

"What's that supposed to mean?" William moved closer to Zaya and she instinctively shrank back. "Did you remember something? Is that where all this is coming from?"

His chair was next to hers, and his bulk crowded her slightly, making her feel claustrophobic. Panic was starting to rise in her, and she clenched her fists to try to control it.

Take a breath, she ordered herself. *I can do this.*

William held a napkin to his face to get the spot of jam that had smeared on his bottom lip, and a memory flashed through her mind. Zaya nearly gasped at how clear it was.

"That first day. I was drugged, but when I came to, there were voices. A crowd of men were in the doorway, their heads and faces covered by a keffiyeh, One of them had a British accent." She pinched her brows together, the wisp of memory fading away. "They called him Blackdown."

Julian looked over at her, his forehead creased in surprise, but he quickly covered it up and turned back to William. "Do you have any idea who or what Blackdown may be?"

He shook his head slowly. "I don't, but I'll definitely look into it." He repositioned to a better angle where he could see Zaya's face straight on. "Do you remember anything else? Any identifying marks on them?"

"The guy with the British accent was around six feet tall, with dark eyes." A shiver ran down her spine remembering how he'd watched her, hands on hips, his black eyes staring a hole through her head. She looked up into William's eyes, their dark depths showing nothing. Had he been there that day? Was it him? She couldn't be sure, but he definitely wasn't ruled out, either. Tears rose in her eyes as she relived that first day of captivity, but she quickly wiped them away.

Julian sensed her distress and reached out to take her hand. She was grateful for the contact, even though she wished it wasn't needed in the first place.

"That's enough for today," he told her. "Why don't you wait for me in the library? I've got a few last things I want to talk about with William." He squeezed her fingers.

She stood, still feeling shaken. "I'm sorry about getting emotional, Chief. Everything is still a little close."

William inclined his head in acknowledgment and she hobbled out of the room, not looking back. Before she'd gone through the doorway, however, she heard William say in a low voice, "You can't keep her safe here, Julian. Let me take her into custody. You know our network. We can protect her."

She slowed her steps, wanting to hear what Julian would say.

"With a mole in your office? I don't think so." Julian's voice was firm.

"I'll personally put her under my protection," William said. "She's our only link to Nazer. Surely you see the logic in letting me take her underground."

"That's one option," Julian replied, sounding so sincere, as if he really might take it under consideration.

The Capture

Zaya wavered for a moment. Was he just trying to bait William, or would he really turn her over to him to prove his guilt? If Nazer was partnering with William, and wanted her dead, her being in William's custody would definitely draw him out. There were a lot of risks in that sort of plan, though. Did Julian think it through, or was he just anxious to capture Nazer?

She walked into the library, shut the door behind her, and went immediately to the window. She needed to feel sunlight on her face. For the last few days, that simple pleasure had become necessary to her feeling of well-being. Her heart rate began to slow as she looked out over the back garden. It was so tranquil, no one would believe a shooting had taken place there an hour before. She leaned her head against the cool glass.

Will there ever be a time I feel truly safe again?

The door opened, and she didn't turn around, assuming Julian had come to find her. "Is Chief Sinclair gone?" she asked, gazing out the window, wishing she were outside.

"Not yet. I'm Deputy Director Aldworth." The man spoke from the doorway, but when she whirled around, he started to advance on her quickly. "We'll be taking you into our custody for your own safety, miss."

Gooseflesh rose on Zaya's arms as he stepped from the shadows into the sunlight and she was able to see his face clearly. Sucking in a breath, she backed up quickly and nearly choked. Those eyes. Dark and evil, staring at her. Just like . . . but no, it couldn't be. The mole was supposed to be William.

The Deputy Director of MI6 couldn't have been there that night with Nazer. Could he?

The room was suddenly too hot. Zaya couldn't breathe. She had to get out. *Keep calm.*

"I need to speak to Commander Bennet first. And I'll need to gather my things." She tried to act casual, but her voice came out breathy and broken. She edged toward the door, but nearly tipped over the chair next to her in her haste to get out. The Deputy Director calmly righted it, effectively blocking her escape.

"I'm afraid I must insist you come with me." His voice was mild, but his eyes flashed with malice. "I can see by your reaction that, in spite of our precautions, you still recognize me. I'm sure you can imagine how damaging that would be if it came out that I had dealings with Mr. al-Raimi. We're going to have to make sure you can't tell anyone." He grabbed her arm and squeezed painfully. "You've been nothing but a trial from the moment I laid eyes on you. Every time we try to silence you, somehow you escape. It's as if nothing short of a stake to the heart will do."

"I seem to recall having a few *trials* of my own, helped along by one of my countrymen. Why? Why would you betray us?" Zaya gulped in air, unable to slow her heartbeat. The last thing she wanted to do was faint in this man's presence.

"We'll have plenty of time to talk on the way to the plane." He pulled her toward him, and she stumbled. A scream started in her throat, but Aldworth caught her and put his hand over her mouth, sticking a knife into her side. "Don't make a sound, or I'll just get it over with now."

She nodded, and he loosened his hold. They started a strange shuffle-drag to the door. Zaya didn't have much time if she hoped to escape with her life. Glancing around the room for anything she could use as a weapon, she mentally cursed. There weren't any knickknacks, and the books were neatly shelved. The small table next to the door had a lamp and a tray on it, the remains of crackers and cheese still visible. That would have to do.

She dragged her feet as they neared the table, hoping for a split second more to reach out and grab the tray. Pushing away from him, she reached out to take it with both hands, grateful it was heavy enough to be real silver. Taking advantage of his surprise, she smashed the tray edge into his throat. He stumbled back, knocking the lamp and table over as he held his windpipe and gasped for air. She immediately grabbed his knife and pointed it at him.

"H-h-how," he wheezed.

She pivoted and used her injured foot to deliver a side kick that drove him to the ground. Triumph surged through her as he groaned, hunched over on the floor, neutralized. She'd protected herself. Taken down a threat. Her training was still there.

Limping to the door, she opened it to see Julian coming down the hall, with William right behind him. "Are you all right? I heard a crash."

She stepped back. "See for yourself."

The men entered the room, and the three of them stared at the man on the floor, attempting to rise. Zaya turned away first. "He's the traitor. I remember now. Deputy Director Aldworth was there. With Nazer." The words came out of her in a rush, so preposterous when she said them out loud, but at the same time, they felt right to put out in the open. "It wasn't William after all."

William turned to them, a stunned look on his face. "You thought I was the mole?"

Julian rubbed his jaw, his complete focus on Aldworth. "We weren't sure. There was some evidence pointing to you, yes." He crossed to the man on the floor and hauled him up. "Do you know what you've done?"

Aldworth still clutched his throat, but he glared at them, resentment pouring off him. "Hopefully I've signed your death warrant," he croaked. He looked toward the ceiling and smiled as they all heard a helicopter approaching.

"Get down!" Julian shouted, dropping Aldworth and running for Zaya. He pulled her with him as they dropped to the floor just as bullets sprayed through the room, the glass from the windows exploding while bullets scarred the floor and walls all around them.

"Don't move," Julian said in her ear, his voice laced with pain.

She tried to twist around to look at him and see if he'd been hit, but he held her fast. Reaching for his fingers, she pulled back when she saw the blood on the back of his hand. "You're hit," she said, trying to push against him to see better.

"A graze," he murmured, his body heavy on hers. The gun barrage had stopped for the moment, and she created enough distance between them that she could look him over. There was so much blood on the front of his shirt she couldn't tell where it was coming from. Panic started to race through her.

He's going to die right in front of me.

Julian was shouting into his comm set. "Tell me we have eyes on this helo and can track it."

Zaya couldn't hear the answer, but knew they had to get out of here. "Come on," she said, pulling Julian with her toward the door. They needed Elliott. Now.

Julian barely moved an inch beyond the desk they had crawled behind before he stopped abruptly. She glimpsed William on the floor. "Chief, are you all right?" She tried to move closer to him, but Julian held her back.

Aldworth rose up in front of them, above the desk, like an avenging angel with a small pistol in his hand, his face bloody. "You're insignificant," he said, wiping blood away from his mouth. "Your pitiful Griffin Force can't stop what's about to happen. To die in the cause means paradise!"

He raised the pistol, but jerked forward as a gunshot rang out. Aldworth slumped over the desk and William stood behind him, his gun still raised. Zaya pulled Julian down and away, checking him over for a new wound.

"You okay, Julian?" the Chief asked, staring at the man he'd just killed.

Julian didn't have time to answer as the helicopter outside began to strafe them again, bullets spraying everywhere. The entire room seemed criss-crossed with ammunition, plaster and wood exploding all around them. Zaya pulled herself as tightly as possible under the desk, Julian's body still shielding her.

When it stopped again, she scrambled out of her hiding place. "Come on," she said to Julian. "Let's go before they come back."

But Julian didn't answer. She looked back to see him kneeling, motionless, staring at William's body a few feet away. He'd been hit several times and was bleeding profusely.

"William," Julian said, his voice anguished as he crawled around the desk to the side of his mentor. He covered the largest wound with both hands, trying to staunch the bleeding. "Elliott, we need you in here," he urgently said into his comm. Even with the scene before him, Julian was steady, but his hand shook as he pressed on the chest wound.

William shook his head. "It's too late," he rasped. "Julian, I have to . . . tell you . . . I never betrayed you. I was loyal to my country. I didn't know about Aldworth, I swear it."

Julian leaned closer to William so he could make out his words. "I know," he reassured the dying man. "We all missed it. Don't waste your energy. When you're better, we'll sort it all out."

"No, no, listen to me." William grabbed Julian's arm. "Aldworth was personally overseeing Atwah's prison transfer. Nazer's come for Atwah. Get to him first." William coughed and more blood pooled under him. "He's leaving Belmarsh. Today. Soon."

Zaya's blood ran cold. Atwah was one of the most dangerous men on the planet and it had taken years to capture him. He'd been the head of the ISIS secret service, with his spies and contacts scattered throughout the world. Atwah himself was like a ghost, quietly taking care of Western "threats" to the spread of ISIS propaganda and overseeing operations that some said resulted in the death of hundreds of people who opposed them.

Julian's attention was riveted to William. "Atwah is in Britain? I would have thought he'd have been transferred to American custody."

"He's in high-security isolation at Belmarsh," William said weakly. "Was trying to radicalize prisoners. Transferring him to Frankland . . . to a separate wing . . . the specialized unit . . . for terrorists."

William wouldn't last much longer. Zaya's heart ached. This man was a legend at Vauxhall Cross as a past field operative. In all of her dealings with him, he'd been gruff, but encouraging. How fitting that his last breaths would be about saving his country from terrorism one more time. How sad he'd had to defend his own honor at the same time.

"We'll take care of this. Don't worry." Julian's shoulders were hunched as he kept up the pressure on William's wound, though he had to know it was a losing battle. "You know I'll take care of everything, I promise."

William's face was ashen. She moved closer. "Thank you for trying to find me, William." She wanted to be strong, but couldn't hold back the tears streaming down her face. "And thank you for saving us today."

"Tell my wife I love her," William said, coughing. "And don't forget how proud I was of you both. Of what you built with Griffin Force. So proud."

Zaya was shoulder to shoulder with Julian, the blood from his own wound running down his arm, his face pale. Was he going into shock?

"Amelia will be looked after, William." Julian's voice broke as he spoke his mentor's name, and Zaya slipped an arm around him, wishing she could freeze time or go back and redo their investigation into the mole—look deeper. Harder.

William glanced between her and Julian, then let his chin fall to his chest. "Take care of each other," he whispered as his eyes rolled back.

Return gunfire sounded outside, and the echoes from the helicopter blades faded. Julian sat on his haunches, his bloody hands in his lap, with his head bowed. "How did I doubt him?" he murmured.

Zaya hugged him to her as they cried for the man they couldn't save, who had died saving them.

Elliott ran in the room, his bag in hand, and quickly surveyed the damage. He didn't say a word as he knelt and checked William's pulse. He pulled out his stethoscope, but the look on his face confirmed what they already knew. "He's g-gone."

Julian stared at his hands covered in blood. "He traded his life for mine."

Zaya squeezed his arm, wanting to take his pain away. "Aldworth planned an attack here today. Admitted his partnership with Nazer." She was still incredulous that he'd pulled off something so brazen.

Glancing over at the body of Aldworth, Julian scowled. "William said they were after Atwah."

"H-he's in England?" Elliott asked, surprise coloring his tone.

"Held at Belmarsh, but getting moved today," Zaya supplied. "Is Augie tracking the helo? I bet they're using that in the attempt to break him out."

"Augie d-didn't say." Elliott moved over to Julian. "Let me l-look at that shoulder."

Julian looked down, as if he'd forgotten he had a bullet wound. "Just give me a butterfly bandage, and I'll be fine."

Elliott sent him a speaking glance. "Not likely. T-take off your shirt."

"Not here." He looked down at William's body. "I . . . We need to take care of him first. Preserve his dignity." He closed his eyes briefly, jaw clenched.

"I'll go find Colt and Jake to h-help." Elliott straightened and bowed his head. "Julian, none of this is your f-fault. Remember that. And it will be w-worth it when we finally c-capture Nazer."

"Nothing could ever be worth this." Julian's face was grim. "Make sure everyone's ready. We're going to Belmarsh."

"Will d-do," Elliott said as he left.

Zaya stood next to Julian and pressed a hand to her throat. "I want to come with you. I need to be there when Nazer's captured."

He looked down at her, his face weary and sad. "That's not a good idea. Too dangerous. Atwah has a network ten times the size of Nazer's—assassins, secret police, and who knows what secrets Aldworth has given them to work with."

"I know, but if I'm ever going to conquer my fears, or change the outcome of my dreams, I have to be there to fight the darkness. Besides, as you keep reminding me, we're a team," she said softly. "We're better together."

He gave her a small smile before he clasped her hand in his and lightly kissed her on the lips. "Always."

The word echoed in her head, and in that moment, she knew she belonged with this man. No matter what obstacles stood between them, they were meant to be together. She reached up to touch his cheek, and emotion rose up inside her. This was where they'd make their stand, to fight Nazer together, and find each other again.

"Let's do this."

CHAPTER SIXTEEN

Julian concentrated on the diamond pattern of the kitchen counter backsplash as Elliott sewed up his bullet wound. He should have taken some pain medicine, but didn't want it to dull his senses. He'd need to be alert for what was coming. Fury filled him as he thought of William's sacrifice, then guilt layered on top of that. How could he have thought William was the traitor? His last act as William's friend and colleague was to accuse him of treason. Julian closed his eyes. With the maelstrom of emotion already storming through him, he definitely didn't need the added cloud of painkillers for his trip to Belmarsh. Nazer's capture depended on his having a clear head.

"Almost done?" he asked Elliott, opening his eyes and trying to look over his shoulder at the wound.

"You're j-just lucky it went straight through. One more s-scar to add to your collection." Elliott methodically worked through the stitches, while Julian tried not to flinch. The burn of the needle going through his skin shimmered over all his nerve endings, but the pain helped him focus. All he could think about was the fact that if it hadn't been for William's quick thinking, he'd be dead—Zaya, too. He'd protected them and lost his life in the process. Julian was going to make sure that counted for something.

"Augie, what have we got?" Julian asked the tech sitting at the table, watching the stitches go in. It was hard to tone down his impatience. He wanted to be out there, tracking Nazer, making sure he didn't slip away again, and this time with Atwah at his side.

Augie bent to his computer, his signature plaid shirt bunching at the shoulders. "The helo did head north toward Belmarsh prison, but he's keeping low, so it's harder to track him." Augie stared at his screen as if it would give him the answers he needed before he could ask the questions. "You know, if he's planning on breaking Atwah out of prison, he'll need more than a helicopter. Security would be heavy for someone like him."

Julian knew Nazer wouldn't attempt this alone. "I'm sure he's got back up. Not only did he have the Deputy Director in his pocket, but Nazer has been courting former al-Qaeda leaders, ISIS and AQIM leaders, and who knows who else, to put himself in the top tier of terrorist leadership. They'd gladly send soldiers to support him in Atwah's escape."

If they had, MI6 would have been the first ones to know. Aldworth probably covered that up, too. Julian's jaw clenched at the possibility of how deep his betrayal had been and how it could affect national security for decades to come. It had taken years to capture Atwah on the Pakistani border, and with the actions of one traitor, Atwah might well escape to wreak havoc again. He would definitely be a powerful ally for Nazer in rebuilding his own organization, after Griffin Force had worked so hard to destroy it.

Julian glanced over at Zaya, who sat in a chair near the door, tapping at her own laptop keyboard. Her face was totally glued to her screen. "What do you think, Z?"

"The child lives in Woolwich," she mumbled, almost to herself, not even looking up.

Julian's frowned at her words. Why was she concentrating on that? "So?"

"Woolwich is close to Thamesmead, where Belmarsh is located. Would Nazer take advantage of his son being so close to the prison?" She looked up for a moment, meeting Julian's eyes. Her brow was still furrowed in concentration. "If he had to choose between them, would he go after the child who's most likely being kept from him or break out Atwah?"

The fact that there was a choice hadn't even occurred to him. "I don't know. I would think Atwah would be his priority." Julian gritted his teeth as Elliott tied off the last stitch. "Do you really think he'd kidnap the child?"

Augie briefly looked up from his screen. "Zaya's guessing he's only known about the child for two years. With Nazer's aspirations of power, and the traditions he adheres to of passing down titles and power from father to son, I think he'd want his son with him." With his hands still paused over his

195

keyboard, he went on. "It's sort of like passing the torch so the child could take over what he started. Not that I understand it, really."

Julian pinched the bridge of his nose. "Let me get this straight. Nazer is attempting to help a man escape that may push him to the forefront as a new leader, bringing together at least three terrorist cells. And we think he's throwing his son in the mix as a possible successor?" Julian's head was starting to throb.

"Exactly." Augie bit his nails as he watched Julian. "But it's just a theory."

"Wonderful." Julian ran a hand over his face. "So do we go to the prison first, as William thought we should, or to Woolwich?"

"My gut tells me he's going straight to Woolwich." Zaya closed her laptop. "But we're an hour away by car. No way we could catch him."

"If I drive, we can make it to Redhill in record time. They have a heliport there, and we'll be right behind Nazer." Julian stood up and winced as he jostled his arm. "Augie, you run the op from here, okay? We'll have a full communications package with us, so you'll be able to see and hear everything in real time."

"Sounds good. I'll just set up in the sitting room instead of the library, because . . ." Augie glanced over at Zaya, his blue eyes wide. "Never mind. Good luck, boss." He packed up his laptop and exited the kitchen, the door closing softly behind him.

Julian walked over to Zaya. "Sure you don't want to stay with him? You've got some skills that could really help from here."

"I have to be there when you capture Nazer." She looked up at him, her gaze steady. "I can handle it."

He nodded, but inside he worried. She was still vulnerable wherever Nazer was concerned, and he wanted to protect her from that. But he also had to trust her. "All right, let's go."

She closed her laptop and they walked into the hall to meet up with the rest of the team. "Ready?" Colt asked, his mouth set in a firm line as he checked his holster one more time.

Jake nodded to Julian, his blue eyes full of sympathy as he handed him his tac gear. "I'm really sorry about William."

"Thanks," Julian said, as he pulled on his vest. "Where's Mya?"

"She's staying behind to run support for Augie and make sure everything is taken care of here." Jake tilted his head toward the library.

Julian got the hint, but didn't let his eyes stray to where William's body still lay until MI6 could retrieve it. It was a small measure of relief that one of the team would be here with William until then. "Thanks." He strode to the front door, Zaya at his side and his team behind. Like old times. How it was always meant to be.

The Capture

As Julian had promised, it didn't take long to get to Redhill Aerodrome, and in minutes, the helicopter he kept there for emergencies was in the air.

"Did we notify RAF Benson?" Julian asked Colt, wanting every base covered.

"Yep. They deployed MK2 helicopters to the prison." Colt sat back, looking confident. "There's no way Nazer will get Atwah into the air, not with a British air fleet and Griffin Force on top of him."

Julian looked over at Zaya. If he were in Nazer's shoes, about to attempt a daring and probably doomed escape attempt, he'd secure his possible successor first. Whether the boy would be in the helicopter with Nazer, or stashed somewhere so he could be spirited out of the country, he would be top priority. "The closer we get, the more I think you're right, Z. Nazer's going to get his son first. That's the only thing that makes sense."

Zaya dipped her head, holding onto the seat as the helicopter performed a steep curve. "Are we going to Woolwich then?"

"Do we have the mother's address?" Julian asked, hoping they did. Not that Augie couldn't get it for them, but they were rushing this op, and there hadn't really been time to think of everything. If they had small details like the address with them, it might be a little sign that fate was on their side.

"Right here." Zaya said, holding a small piece of paper.

Julian smiled and took it from her. That was exactly the sign he needed. Zaya was always prepared. He'd once teased her on their first missions together that the Boy Scout motto was "be prepared," and the Zaya motto was "always prepared." She'd grinned and told him he surprised her with flashes of inspiration every now and then.

"Where will we land?" she asked, looking at the scenery blurred below them.

"The closest place would be the Royal Artillery Barracks. It's only a five minute drive to Caroline's flat from there." Julian was still amazed that Zaya had put it together that they were laundering money through child support payments. The Vista building where the mother lived in Woolwich wouldn't be anything luxurious. Likely a one or two bedroom flat—definitely not the lap of luxury needing the amount of money being deposited in her account. From what he knew of Woolwich, she'd probably been hiding from Nazer and trying to blend in, not realizing the extent of Nazer's reach.

"Has anyone let the Minister of Defence know we're landing at the Artillery Barracks? I'd hate to get shot down on our own soil," Jake said with a wry grin.

"All taken care of. Soldiers are meeting us on the ground with support vehicles. News of William is already starting to spread. Everyone wants Nazer captured and Atwah to stay right where he is." Julian faced forward. They had to have Nazer in custody today. This was their make-or-break moment, he could feel it.

The Capture

The moment they set down, the team disembarked from the helicopter and left it in the hands of the soldiers who were waiting, before heading for the two cars nearby. The adrenaline was starting to flow fast, and Julian was more than ready to get going and take Nazer down.

They all paused in a huddle near the first car, to go over the op once more. "Jake, if we're going to box him in, I'll take Zaya and Colt with me down Wellington Street with a turn onto John Wilson. You take Nate and Elliott, keep going on Wellington and turn on Thomas." Julian took one last look at the GPS, pointing to the different routes.

Jake nodded. "Copy that. Be careful," he said, before he ducked inside.

Julian got in the second car, and Zaya slid into the passenger side. "Do you have a plan for when we get there?" she asked. "Or are we winging it?"

"Half and half." He gave her a rueful half-grin. "So far, my plan is to approach Caroline and tell her she needs protection for herself and her son. Jake and Nate will back me up." He pulled the car onto the road. "Then we wait for Nazer."

"And you'll have me, too." Zaya pulled out the communications case and opened it, a little frown appearing on her face. "This doesn't look like the package we used six months ago."

"It isn't." Julian suppressed a frustrated sigh on her behalf. There was so much she'd missed, but shouldn't have.

This time pushing the guilt away was easier, though. He was making progress.

"This is new technology. The earpiece is pretty much the same, just sits a little deeper in the ear canal. That small wire there," he nodded toward the bottom of the case, "is a tiny camera you can attach to the button on your shirt. It provides continuous feed of what you're seeing."

"Sounds easy enough." She shifted the case on her lap, studying it and not meeting Julian's eyes.

"It is," he assured her, feeling her discouragement at being behind. She just needed a bit of time to catch up, that's all.

After pulling to the curb a block away from Caroline's apartment, he leaned over and took the case, putting in an earpiece and attaching the camera to the top of his body armor. "All of this is configured for both your laptop and Augie's, so you can see and hear what's going on."

She hesitated for a heartbeat before she reached out and touched his cheek. His skin warmed at her touch. "Be careful," she told him, worry in her tone.

He smiled, his heart thumping harder that she was worried about him. With a light kiss on her lips, he opened his door. "I'll be right back."

With one last glance, he got out of the car and adjusted his tactical gear. "Colt, you fan out to the side. Jake, are you and Nate in position?"

"Affirmative," came Jake's reply over his earpiece. "We're in the rear of the building. Looks quiet."

The Capture

Julian moved forward, his eye on the front door of the apartments as he moved toward the side doors. Everything was so ordinary-looking and quiet. Had they guessed wrong? Was Nazer on his way to Belmarsh and not headed here at all? "I'm moving in."

He stole carefully over to the Vista building, but before he could turn the corner to the side entrance, the front door swung open. The man he'd hunted for the better part of two years stepped out, holding a young boy's hand. Julian quickly moved for cover, but Nazer spotted him and immediately picked up the child.

"Commander Bennet." The words came out as an exasperated grunt. "Don't come any closer."

Julian had his hand on his gun, but he didn't want to frighten the kid or escalate the situation faster. "Put him down and let me take you in quietly. No need for the child to get hurt."

Nazer shook his head, pointing his gun toward Julian. "He won't. We're leaving. Now back away."

A woman flew out of the apartment building doors. "Give me back my son," she wailed as she ran toward Nazer. He whipped the boy to his other arm, and the child cried out, but Nazer ignored him and backed up, his gun pointed toward the child's head.

"Both of you back off or this ends right now."

"You're scaring him. Can you at least lower your weapon?" Julian asked, anxious to keep him talking. In all of Nazer's operations, one thing investigators noted was how calm and collected he always was, but right now his gun was shaking in his hand. "Let's all take a breath and think things through," Julian continued.

"I've thought everything through." Nazer moved the boy aside slightly, so Julian could see wires and small canisters poking out from his vest. "I've served my purpose, and now it's time to have my reward. In paradise. To become the celebrated martyr I was meant to be, my son at my side."

"No!" Caroline's cry was barely a croak. "Don't do this. Please. Let him go."

"Nazer, you've wanted to take me down for years. Here's your chance. Let the boy go. Take me in his place," Julian said, his mouth dry. The terror on the mother's face was impossible to witness and not want to do something. He couldn't just stand there.

"You don't deserve a martyr's death," Nazer sneered, as he backed up a little more.

"If you won't take Commander Bennet, take me." Zaya's voice came from the street. Julian's heart stuttered as stark fear washed over him, immobilizing every muscle in his body. What was she doing out of the car?

"No!" he said sharply, his voice loud in his own ears. "Zaya, stand down."

"I can't, Julian. You know I can't." Zaya's voice trembled, but she didn't look at anyone but the child in Nazer's arms.

The Capture

A cruel smile lit Nazer's face as he looked between Zaya and Julian. "Come," he said, motioning to Zaya. "Let's negotiate terms."

Nazer wouldn't negotiate. Zaya knew that as well as he did. "Stay where you are," Julian said to Zaya, a thread of pleading in his voice. She didn't listen, and it was agony watching Zaya move slowly toward him. The after-effects of her nightmares ran through his head, her panic about ever being in Nazer's custody again and suffering through more torture and starvation.

And now she was walking into her own nightmare.

"Hurry." Nazer pulled the boy closer, and his mother whimpered from a few feet away.

Zaya walked forward. Her lips were moving, though she was too far away for either him or Nazer to hear what she was saying. As soon as the thought registered, however, he heard her whisper coming through his earpiece. "It'll be okay. If this is how I'm supposed to conquer my demons, then so be it. I don't want anyone to suffer at his hand ever again."

Her words stirred him to action. He moved toward Zaya's position. He understood her reasoning, but there weren't going to be any martyrs here today. Not if he could help it.

CHAPTER SEVENTEEN

*Z*aya kept her eyes on the little boy who was sobbing uncontrollably and reaching for his mother. That's what kept her moving forward. If she looked at the man holding him, she'd lose her composure completely. Her heart was pounding so hard against her ribs, she could hardly catch her breath. She limped forward, feeling Julian's eyes on her. Hopefully someday he'd understand why she had to do this.

Dr. Finch's words echoed through her head as she struggled to breathe. *Focus on your breaths until you feel in control. In. Out. Focus.*

Out of the corner of her eye, Julian took a step toward her, but Nazer's voice rang out with the one threat that held any sway. "Stay where you are, Commander, or there won't be anything left of us beyond a stain on the pavement."

The boy's cries grew louder, his anguished face nearly a mirror of his mother's, brown eyes wide and filled with tears. Nazer seemed oblivious to the boy's pain and just tilted his head away from the frightened child's screams.

Her heart couldn't bear the scene. His terrified screams shot straight to her core. With firsthand knowledge of Nazer's cruelty, she would spare this child if she could. It wasn't ideal, obviously, and she hadn't been able to tell Julian her plan to offer herself in trade, but as a precaution, she'd taken a comm set with an earpiece and camera as well. So, while she'd be in Nazer's custody once again, this time, Julian could find her, and she would do everything in her power to make sure the boy was safe.

When she was within a few feet of Nazer, she stopped. "Give the boy to his mother."

He twisted his lips into a condescending half-smile, as if she were a small child herself who didn't understand the grownups around her. "You don't give the orders here."

Motioning her closer, he made sure she was within arm's reach before he backed away, leading Zaya farther from Julian. "Commander, it seems providence wants to teach you a lesson I couldn't teach you on my own. Soon you'll know what it feels like to lose everyone you care about. To see your every dream go up in smoke."

Zaya was concentrating so hard on Nazer, she didn't see the car speeding toward them until it was almost on top of their little group. Gunshots came from behind them, pinging all around Julian's position. Zaya hit the ground, her hands over her head. Julian returned fire, but it was too late. Nazer was already dragging Zaya and the child into the car, cursing the entire way. Zaya was frozen, her body instinctively pulling away from

Nazer with her flight or fight response. But his arms were like metal bands, restraining her until she was pinned and unable to do anything else but get in the car. She heard Julian calling her name from far away, and for a moment thought she might lose consciousness.

Instead, she concentrated on breathing, and on the child's hand in hers. As soon as the three of them were crammed in the back seat, the tires squealed, and the driver took off like a shot. Zaya looked back through the window to see Julian's panicked face running towards the car.

"It's okay." She swallowed the sob rising in her throat and murmured into the embedded microphone covering the top button on her shirt. "Please find me."

Nazer heard her words, but thankfully he didn't suspect she was speaking into a comm set. He shook his head. "No matter how much you will it, wish it, or pray for it, the commander won't find you before your time has come."

The little boy was between them, wailing until he couldn't catch a breath. She drew him closer. "Shh, it's all right," she told him as she rubbed his back. "Don't cry."

"I want to go home," he hiccuped into her shirt. "Please."

"You will. Soon." She pushed his hair back from his forehead and gave him a smile, hoping she was telling him the truth.

Nazer gave a derisive snort, meeting her eyes over the little boy's head. "I should have killed you when I had the chance," he said, staring at her. "But you impressed me. Day after day. You never broke. And all over some misplaced loyalty to a man who didn't deserve it."

Zaya felt rage rising within her, but shoved it down. She had to stay clear-headed. "Where are you taking us?"

"To paradise. Now be quiet." He leaned back in his seat and picked up his phone. He pressed a button, then held it to his ear. Speaking in Arabic, he asked the person on the other end if "it" was done and scowled at the answer.

Had his plan to break Atwah out of prison failed? Zaya suppressed a smile. Good. One less weapon Nazer would have at his disposal. She glanced at the suicide vest. If she could defuse it, they would definitely be on more equal footing. But, the trigger switch connecting to the wires looked complicated and besides, he'd never let her close enough. She had to be patient and think of another way to get out of this alive.

He met her gaze again, and she turned away. After hanging up, he shifted in his seat to face her and the boy more fully.

"You know, when I first took you in Morocco, I had no idea how important you were to Commander Bennet." His low tone was conversational, melodic, and nearly hypnotizing in the right circumstances. In that moment, she was transported back to a small cell, listening to that slightly accented voice right before she was caned. Her entire body wanted to shut down and cry being back in his custody, but she dug her nails into her palms to keep herself in the present. She was going to see this through.

Nazer looked into her soul, as if he could see her fear and multiply it with his words. "I'm surprised you would offer yourself to me again."

"It was supposed to be a trade, but of course you went back on your word." She lifted her chin. "I should have expected that. You have no honor."

He made a clucking sound. "What would you know of honor? I'm sure Commander Bennet understood what happened. And I admit, I enjoyed his look of pain when he saw you next to me." He shifted his legs apart. "Last year, my spies found circumstantial evidence that the two of you were involved, but it wasn't until you went to Morocco that I knew. And the plan was set in motion to abduct you and make sure Commander Bennet would never know what happened to you. How unfortunate for him that so soon after he got to play hero, you were lost to him again. I won't be so careless with you this time."

She clenched her hands to stop their shaking and focus her thoughts as she faced him. "What are you talking about?"

"I know you are *very* important to Commander Bennet." The hard slash of his mouth curved into a smile. "I didn't believe it at first, not until he made arrangements to buy you a unique engagement ring when you were in Morocco. That was my window to snatch you away. It was almost too easy."

Zaya's mind was trying to catch up, to process his words. All those months she'd wondered where Julian had gone that day, why he'd been so secretive, and he'd been buying her an engagement ring? No wonder he was crushed with guilt. A little thrill shot through her at the thought of Julian proposing, but she squashed it quickly, not wanting Nazer to see any reaction from her. "I don't believe you."

Nazer shrugged. "What you believe is of no consequence to me. But your continued loyalty to Bennet quickly became tiresome. I would have killed you months ago, but I enjoyed torturing the commander with losing you. I had the woman he wanted to marry. He couldn't find you, much less save you. It was a glorious feeling: giving him a taste of helplessness, having someone steal the woman who should have been by his side if not for his negligence."

She schooled her features to present a blank face, as if she didn't care what he was saying. "It seems so personal for you. Why do you hate the commander so much?"

"Who doesn't hate the hunter who gives them no peace?" He stared out the window. "But none of that matters now. I will find peace with the other martyrs who have gone before me."

"Ask him where." Julian's voice was soft in her ear, and she nearly gasped in relief. He was there with her. A feeling of strength surged through her veins.

"Have you chosen a place for your martyrdom then?" she asked, trying to keep her voice nonchalant.

"Not only mine, but yours, as well," he said, reaching over to touch the top of the little boy's head between them. "Since my son can no longer have the power and authority he's entitled to, he will come with me to a place of honor. You, of course, won't be there with us, since you're a dishonorable woman, but I can't very well let you live."

"So, you're going to kill all of us for your own selfish reasons. Very predictable." She pressed the little boy's head closer to her body, not wanting Nazer's hands near either of them and wishing she could shield him from what was happening. "Just this once, could you think of someone else? He's your son. Let him go," she spoke quietly, hoping Nazer might respond to a soft plea. "Please. He's five years old and has his whole life ahead of him."

"A boy needs his father." He reached for the child's hand, but he shrank back, curling into a ball as much as their position would allow. Nazer touched his chin. "Hadi, you will understand someday."

He raised his head, his brown eyes red-rimmed from crying. "My name is Hugh."

"You are meant for great things, and after today your name, Hadi al-Raimi, will be known throughout the world." He pulled the boy toward him, but he resisted with every ounce of energy his little body had.

"No. My name is Hugh Alden." He squirmed out of Nazer's grip and pressed back against the seat.

Nazer stared at the child, anger flitting across his features, but he quickly painted a superficial smile on his face instead, then gave up and looked out the window. "We're almost there."

211

The Capture

Zaya looked at her surroundings. "Almost where?" They were near a bunch of warehouses. Hopefully her camera was picking up some of this.

"In Afghanistan, you weren't half as chatty," Nazer commented. "I must remind you to hold your tongue. As I recall, you didn't care for the consequences for disobedience."

His tone was mild, but she knew the cruelty he was capable of. Looking at the warehouses, she shivered, remembering the different prisons he'd kept her locked in not long ago. She didn't want to go back to dark places or have to face any of Nazer's consequences.

Julian can find me, she reminded herself. And she had a little boy who needed her to stay calm.

The car stopped near a large warehouse that had seen better days. At first, Zaya thought they were all going into the building, but then she saw a second car near the corner. A swarthy-looking small man stood next to it, his arms folded as he waited.

Nazer got out, motioning for Zaya and Hugh to do the same. She debated disobeying, but knew she couldn't outrun him with her injuries. Her choices were limited, and Julian was still their best chance of getting out of this. She just had to be patient.

They approached the man by the second car, while the driver that brought them there drove off without a backward glance.

"What's the status?" Nazer said to the new driver in Arabic.

"The authorities were waiting at Belmarsh." The man stood straight, as if Nazer was his military superior, but he didn't salute. "We failed."

"We won't fail now." Nazer gently patted the vest. "We will be taking two more initiates with us."

The man flicked his gaze over Zaya and Hugh, but didn't look happy about their new status. "Have they been swept for tracking devices?"

Nazer pulled Zaya forward. "There wasn't time."

The little man took a small wand out of his coat pocket and swept it over her. The beeping was steady until it got to her camera button. "She's transmitting from this." He pulled the short camera wire free from her shirt, ripping the top button off.

Nazer took the wire, frowning at her, before dropping it to the ground and crushing the camera with his foot. "I should have guessed." He motioned for the man to finish.

The contents of Zaya's stomach roiled. All she had left connecting her to Julian was her earpiece. It was deeper into her ear than the ones she'd had six months ago, so hopefully that would prevent its discovery. Even the thought of Julian not having any way to find her again made her mouth go dry. The wand beeped steadily over the rest of her body and head, but she didn't breathe a sigh of relief until the man had finished near her ears and stepped back.

"She's clean." He put the wand back into his pocket. "If we're going to keep to the schedule, we must leave now."

Zaya drew her eyebrows down in confusion. There was a schedule when you were going to martyr yourself? That seemed strange, but Zaya was silent.

Nazer took his son by the arm and marched toward the car. Zaya followed, Hugh's frightened face the only thing keeping her focused.

Julian will be here soon, she kept chanting over and over in her head. They'd get through this.

"Zaya, I'm still here. You can hear me, and I can hear you." Julian's voice was in her ear, soft and comforting. "We're coming for you. Almost there."

How could she stall? She slowed her steps. "My foot . . ." She winced. "I just need a minute. It hurts."

Nazer barely glanced at the driver, but even without an audible order, the little man immediately moved to Zaya's side and grabbed her elbow, propelling her along. "Get in the car."

He hustled her into the back seat, where Nazer and Hugh waited. Had that been enough time? How far out was Julian?

The driver didn't waste a minute and quickly drove away, headed toward London. Zaya tried to make her voice casual, to give Julian a heads up that they were moving and what direction they were going. "You know, if we're going into the city, it might be faster to take Rotherhithe New Road."

"Shut up," Nazer said. "We don't need any advice from you."

"Clever girl," Julian said in her ear, and she breathed in. He was close; she could feel it.

The traffic was slowing, but Nazer didn't seem anxious. He watched Hugh closely, as if memorizing the details of the boy's face. She couldn't imagine what he was thinking, and probably didn't want to. What person in their right mind would take their child to a suicide bombing?

Nazer was shifting quite a bit, as if he couldn't find a comfortable position. Zaya crossed her ankles and looked over at him. "Do you need to loosen your vest?" Maybe if he allowed her to help, she could get a closer look at it.

He gave her a suspicious glance. "If you're trying to find a way to get it off me, you won't find one. It's connected to my vital signs. If it stops detecting my heartbeat, or if my breathing slows, the bomb will go off. You should be hoping I stay alive until we're in position."

"You're a bad man," Hugh said softly, staring up into his father's eyes.

"If you'd had a chance to get to know me, you wouldn't say that," Nazer snapped, bending to be face to face with Hugh. "Your mother hid you from me, but as soon as I found out about you, I wanted to know you. I sent you letters with my presents. Did you read them?"

"I never got any presents or letters." The boy looked confused now. "Did you send them to my house?"

Nazer's hands clenched in his lap. "Your mother never gave them to you?"

The boy glanced between Zaya and Nazer, bewilderment on his face. "Why wouldn't she give me my presents?"

"I'm sure she had her reasons," Zaya said, trying to soothe him. How would she feel if her son's father were one of the most wanted terrorists in the world? Hugh's mother was obviously struggling to deal with that fact as well, and how much her son should know about his birth father.

"There are no valid reasons to keep a son from his father," Nazer said firmly. "She will always remember that now."

Zaya thought of the mother's hysterical cries. Her life was forever changed, and so was her son's. Would either of them recover? She shook her head, angry at how many people were being hurt, that this woman was another casualty of Nazer's reign of horror. "The boy doesn't deserve this. Can't you let him go?"

"My son will follow me to paradise since I was denied the privilege of raising him properly here. And why would I care what you say? This is a parent's decision." Nazer turned back to look out the window. "The only reason you are here is so Commander Bennet will learn *his* lesson once and for all. He has hunted me, tortured me, tried to wipe me off the face of the earth. And for that, I will take his peace from him. I will take you."

Zaya was incredulous. She leaned forward and fixed her gaze on him. "How has he tortured you?" Did he really think of himself as a victim? She held out her palms so he could see the scars. "You had me caned, starved, and beaten. You're the one who tortures people, not the other way around."

216

Nazer pulled up his sleeve to his forearm, revealing skin that was puckered and pink. "I've been burned, shot, and beaten. Your commander is not innocent in this business. He's so sure of his righteousness, but he's more similar to me than he thinks. We both chase the power that comes with position, no matter the cost."

"You're wrong," Zaya said with a shake of her head. "Julian Bennet has worked hard to save people from men like you. He's done whatever it took to make that happen, yes, but he could walk away from his position at any time. Once he has you in custody, in a high-security prison where you'll never see freedom again, his job is over. He's done."

Nazer laughed, shaking his head in amusement. "You're naïve. No man could walk away from that kind of money and power."

"Commander Bennet can." She sat back in her seat and folded her arms. "You've tortured and killed so many, that you've probably lost track, all in your quest for power. You're nothing alike."

Nazer grabbed her chin so fast she didn't have time to react. He squeezed until she whimpered. "He's killed more than his fair share. He's bribed officials. Beaten men unconscious for confessions and information. He's no saint."

"Don't touch me." Her entire body was trembling as she tried to pull away. The feel of his hand made her skin crawl. Adrenaline was rushing through her so hard, she couldn't think of anything beyond getting away from him. She clawed at his hand. "Let go of me!"

Nazer shoved her away and turned to look out the window again. "Why am I even trying to reason with a woman?"

Zaya gulped in breaths as she tried to calm herself. Hugh took her shaking hand and whispered, "Are you all right?"

She mustered a smile and nodded. "I'm fine." But she could barely control the impulse to open the door and jump out. She had to fight it, somehow force back the darkness threatening to overwhelm her. Jumping out of the car would only sign a death warrant for both her and Hugh. Instead, she leaned down and smelled the apple-scented shampoo on his little head. Breathing the innocent scent into her nostrils calmed her a bit, and drove away the dread inching through her. She held his little hand tighter. "We're going to be okay. I promise."

"I'll make sure you keep that promise," Julian said in her ear. "I won't let anything happen to you."

But as Zaya looked at the terrorist holding them captive, her heart knew that this time, even Julian might not be able to save them from what Nazer had planned.

CHAPTER EIGHTEEN

Julian could hardly think, his entire focus on Zaya's voice in his ear. He'd spent so long looking for her and hadn't had nearly enough time with her. And now there was a chance he'd lose her again.

No, he thought. *I can't let that happen.*

He murmured Augie's name into his throat mic. "Anything?"

"I'm trying to access traffic cams or satellite coverage to pinpoint the car, but all I have so far is a brief glimpse before Nazer smashed Zaya's camera. You'd be surprised how many black town cars are on the road right now."

Augie's voice had an intensity to it that Julian hadn't heard before. They'd been together through a lot of missions, but it was easy to see that this one was personal for more than just Julian. "Thanks, Augie."

"We'll find her, boss."

"I know." The last clue she'd given stuck in his mind. "What's along Rotherhithe New Road? What could it lead to that would be Nazer's target?" Julian asked aloud, almost to himself.

Augie answered anyway. "Nothing, but that road connects to a hub of others that could take him to Tower Bridge, Southbank Centre, the London Eye, and the Imperial War Museum." They could hear furious keyboard tapping. "Has he turned off somewhere? That would help us get his general direction."

"Z would have said so, if they had." If she could. His heart had nearly stopped beating when he'd heard her say, "Don't touch me." After all that Nazer had done to her already, he didn't deserve to breathe the same air, never mind think he could touch her. Zaya had just started her recovery and now . . . How big of a setback would this be? All he knew is he had to get her out of it.

"He'll choose the most populated place that would make a statement," Colt said from the back seat. "Any of those places would fit the bill, but I'm leaning more toward the Tower Bridge or London Eye."

"Which one would make the most impact if attacked?" Jake said. "All of those locations have tight security."

"The Tower Bridge may make sense as the target," Augie put in. "At this time of day, a lot of people would be there."

"And an explosion on the bridge would be dramatic." Colt swiped a hand across his forehead. "Nazer wants to be remembered."

It would be beyond difficult to try and stop an attack on the bridge in such a high traffic area. Julian pinched the bridge of his nose. What could he do?

When Nazer's voice came over their earpieces, they all quieted. "In some ways, it's fitting that you'll be there to witness my martyrdom—a Griffin Force agent, one of the hunters, dying with the hunted."

"The moment you leave this world, your name will be forgotten. You're just a blip on the radar of history." Zaya's voice was strong, which made Julian feel better.

"I will be remembered as one of the great men who fought in the jihad against the Great Satan." His voice was smooth, but Julian could detect an edge creeping in. They had to get them before Nazer could get to the location he'd chosen.

"You're no bin Laden," she said to Nazer. Her voice sounded so close; Julian wished she really was next to him. Instead, she was sitting with a man who had no conscience. "And everyone knows you can only aspire to leadership. Besides, isn't blowing yourself up the same as admitting defeat? Griffin Force will win and so will everyone else who's worked to bring you to justice."

"We'll see who is remembered and who is not," Nazer snapped back. "And Commander Bennet won't be gloating over my death, since he'll spend the rest of his life mourning yours."

Julian's fists clenched. Nazer had pegged him there. He couldn't imagine ever getting over Zaya. "Can we go any faster?" he asked Jake softly, not wanting to speak over the conversation in Nazer's car.

"Doing my best, boss, but traffic is a mess this time of day." Even so, he changed lanes and sped up, dodging a few cars and earning a honk or two in return.

"Commander Bennet won't mourn my death the rest of his life," Zaya continued. "He'll move on, but he'll be able to look back and remember the love we had. That's more than I can say for you."

She was wrong about that. Moving on wouldn't be part of the equation for Julian. But her words made him think that maybe she was trying to give him a subtle goodbye. It was more than he could bear. He clenched his fists and closed his eyes, sending up a silent prayer.

Please let me find her.

Nazer's voice filled his ears in answer. "You don't need love when you have respect. That's why I've chosen this place to spend my final moments on earth and make my point clear to those left behind." There was some rustling and then silence.

Julian held his breath.

"Why would you choose the Imperial War Museum?" Zaya's voice was loud and clear.

The air whooshed out of Julian as the last puzzle piece clicked into place. The War Museum. Where dozens of schoolchildren and tourists would be walking around learning about wars of the past. And having a new war brought up close and personal if Nazer detonated that vest.

"This country memorializes the wars they've started and the people they've murdered. I'm going to make sure they remember the day when war was brought to their doorstep."

Julian leaned forward and turned to the other team members in his car as another shot of adrenaline went through him. "Mr. al-Raimi has severely underestimated us. Which is brilliant, actually. Let's show him how *we're* going to remember this day," he said, a sense of urgency filling him.

Hang on, Z, he thought, imagining her face filled with trust for him. *I'm coming.*

CHAPTER NINETEEN

Zaya looked at the busload of schoolchildren about to enter the side entrance of the Imperial War Museum. Could she warn them? One glance at Nazer's determined face told her she couldn't. Closing her eyes, she slid her arm around Hugh's small shoulders. This was an impossible situation.

They got out of the car, the driver following discreetly behind them, but he broke off before they entered. It seemed he wasn't going to be a martyr along with them today. As soon as he left, Nazer changed position, pulling Hugh's head snug against his side, so if anything happened, Hugh would be in the middle of it. Zaya's only consolation was that Julian knew where they were. He just had to get there in time.

Following the stream of schoolchildren being admitted through the side door, they joined the throng. No one at the entrance questioned their presence with the class, not even the security guard. With the overcast day, Nazer's baggy jacket wouldn't be questioned, and he looked like every other parent on a field trip with their child. Everyone on the museum staff smiled at the excited children laughing and talking with their school friends, not even suspecting a bomb was about to go off in their midst.

Once through the door, they approached a fire alarm. Zaya thought she might be able to reach over and pull it. The moment the alarm rang, the Museum would start an evacuation procedure, but Nazer's hand snaked out and grabbed her arm. "No. Not until there's something for the fire trucks to do. Try to warn anyone again, and I'll just detonate where we stand. More innocent blood will be on your hands."

Zaya glared at him, but he ignored her and continued toward the middle of the museum. There was a small observation deck where guests could look down at an open floorspace below with large displays, including a tank and rocket, or look up to several terraced floors with different exhibits on each one. Beyond that, framed in the glass atrium ceiling above them, airplanes from bygone eras hung.

"Up to the third floor," Nazer told her, nudging her arm. "Quickly."

"What's on the third floor?" she asked, wanting to give Julian a clue as to their location, but also genuinely curious. What would make Nazer pick this museum for his "martyrdom."

"There is a presentation memorializing the attacks on my countrymen. One of your country's experts, Major General John Thomson is speaking on why they invaded Afghanistan and slaughtered innocents," he said with disdain. "Although I'm sure he'll couch it differently. No matter how he lies, the truth is, he was part of the Joint Command and bears responsibility for what happened there at the hands of the U.S. and Britain."

Zaya shuddered. The more he talked, the worse this sounded. Heading up two flights of stairs, she looked around at the crowded halls of teachers, students, and tourists.

Run, she wanted to scream to them. *Get out.*

But she stayed silent, knowing Nazer could detonate his vest at any time.

Hurry, Julian, she thought.

Hugh had glued himself to her side, and she frantically looked for some miracle, a way to escape the situation without anyone dying. Around her were all the mementoes from war and its effect on people's lives. A mangled car. A tank. Vintage warplanes. Guns and a rocket. It was ironic that Nazer had chosen a place that showcased exhibits about the wars of the past, so horrors like that would never happen again, yet it was about to happen right in front of them.

Walking to the lecture room, she knew she had to think fast. This was her last chance to do something before Nazer detonated the vest. But all around her were glass cases filled with war artifacts and TVs playing films about soldiers of the past. Nothing that could provide protection from Nazer or give her a way out.

Turning the last corner, Zaya noticed fewer and fewer people, as if the stream of tourists and schoolchildren had suddenly been cut off. Suddenly a voice rang out from somewhere below them.

The Capture

"Nazer al-Raimi!"

Julian.

Zaya's heart soared, but then it sank at the realization that tactically, the only reason Julian would reveal himself was to provide a distraction while an evacuation took place. Now Nazer would have the chance to kill them both.

Nazer stopped, then slowly turned around, taking the few steps back to the nearest observation deck. He peered down at the first floor, yanking her close to him. "Commander Bennet, how lovely of you to come today." He leaned close to her ear, and she jerked away. He smirked at her reaction, glancing down at Julian. "I guess I didn't find all the trackers you had, did I? Where is it?" He grabbed her arm and shook her hard. "Give it to me now."

Zaya took out the comm piece from her ear and mutely handed it over.

"There will be consequences for all of us now," Nazer said, as he threw it over the side of the railing.

Blood drained from her face as his words registered, but with the empty hallways and open floor plan, she could hear the shuffle of people being herded out of the building. No matter what happened or when the bomb went off, hopefully the children would be far away. A sliver of triumph went through her. A lot of lives would be saved today. Terror would never claim total victory.

"You can't win now, Nazer. You might as well give up."

Nazer pushed her away and gripped Hugh's arm. His eyes focused on the door of the room where the Major General was to speak. "Come on," he said, over his shoulder to her. "I know you want to see this through."

He opened the door, but the room was empty. "The coward!" Nazer muttered angrily. He took out his gun and swept the room before he pointed it at Zaya. "Where did they take him?" he demanded, as if Zaya were somehow responsible.

"I don't know." Zaya shrank back, not liking the crazed look in his eye.

"Do you know how to say anything other than that? That's all I've heard from you for months." He started to pace, waving his gun as he talked. "You're going to help me find him." But he shook his head. "And do exactly as I say."

He looked like he was losing his grip on reality. Not good when he was wearing a powerful bomb on his chest. Hugh wiggled free of Nazer's hand and looked like he wanted to run. That scenario had too many variables, so she pulled Hugh closer to her. "We will."

Nazer took Zaya's arm and dragged both her and Hugh along with him back to the observation deck. He looked down to the last place they'd seen Julian, and pushed the gun painfully into her side as they leaned over the waist-high safety glass.

The main floor was eerily empty now. Considering the room had nearly been at capacity when they came in, Zaya felt a measure of satisfaction go through her that so many people were safely away. But the tension radiating from Nazer gave her pause. There was still a good chance she and Hugh wouldn't get away from here unscathed. The little boy had started crying again, and his wails were an ominous background to the scene playing out before them.

"Commander Bennet, show yourself," Nazer ordered.

"Let her go first." Julian didn't come out in the open this time, but his voice echoed through the atrium, around the tank and aircraft that had once protected soldiers like him.

"We will all die together," Nazer said. "However, *I* will go into the light of Allah with my son." He reached down to touch Hugh's shoulder, as if to reassure himself he that was still there, but his gaze stayed on the main floor, searching for Julian. "No matter what you do, your tactics will not drive away the freedom fighters."

"Is that what you call yourself?" Julian laughed, scornfully. "A freedom fighter? When you order people to be tortured or watch men, women, and children be beaten? Is that how you sleep at night—calling yourself a freedom fighter?"

"I could ask you the same question, commander." Nazer backed away, pulling her deeper into the shadows. Zaya resisted, but Nazer dug the gun into her side so hard she cried out. There was no choice but to follow. "You say you are fighting terrorists, but you invade countries, kill innocents, and then act surprised when we fight back."

"I'm not the one holding a woman and child hostage." Julian's voice came from the right. Nazer moved swiftly away, heading for the other side of the atrium.

"If you're such a hero, why don't you show your face?" Nazer taunted. They were near the staircase that led down to the first floor of the atrium where Julian and the team would be waiting.

Stay hidden, Julian, she thought, hoping he could somehow key in to what she was thinking.

But Julian didn't hear her plea, and neither did the rest of the team. Colt, Jake, Brenna, and Julian all stepped forward in different areas of the main floor, the sunlight streaming through the windows onto these people who had suffered unimaginable things because of Nazer al-Raimi.

"We're all here, Nazer. Look into the faces of the men and women who brought you down." Julian stared up at Nazer and Zaya from his vantage point on the first floor, and her heart stopped. There was a look of intensity on his face she'd never seen before, his eyes boring into hers, telling her all the things he couldn't say.

Tears pricked her eyes at how courageous he was standing there in the open, sacrificing everything for her. She loved him. She'd never stopped.

As if Nazer could squash the feelings of her heart, he pulled her closer, making sure the team below could see them. "How fortunate for all of you to be here today to witness the death of this loyal team member," he said loudly, as he held the gun to her temple. "Maybe I should do that first, before I detonate the vest."

"No." Julian held up his hands, then let his arm that held his gun fall to his side, leaving him completely unprotected. "Let her go," he said firmly, holding out his hands palms up. "This is between the two of us. No one else has to get hurt."

"Don't," Zaya said with a shake of her head. "Don't do this for me."

"How noble," Nazer sneered. "Trying to appear the hero at the end." Changing tactics, Nazer pointed his gun straight at Julian. "I could shoot you right now, and even if every one of your team members shoots me, the bomb will detonate the moment my heart stops and Zaya will join me in death after all. Either way, I win."

"Why don't you stop hiding behind a woman? Come down here and face me like a man," Julian said, the frustration in his voice echoing off the walls.

Zaya watched the exchange between the two men, wondering why Julian was staying exposed. The rest of the team changed positions every so often, and Nazer had a hard time keeping them all in sight. It didn't make any sense until she realized that they were distracting him. Whatever plan was in place, Zaya knew this was her opportunity to help Julian save them all.

Hugh stood next to her, his sobs still raw, but they had subsided somewhat. She pulled his trembling hand behind her, inching him away from Nazer. If she could maneuver just right, they might have this one chance to escape. Putting a little more distance between her and Hugh so he wouldn't be hurt if this went bad, she carefully moved her hand closer to the gun Nazer held loosely in his left hand. He leaned over the safety wall and concentrated on Julian, his entire focus on the scene below. The perfect distraction.

Quick as lightning she grabbed the gun, but his hand reflexively clenched around it. They started an arm wrestle for it, and Nazer squeezed the trigger twice, hitting the safety glass between them and the three floors below.

"Zaya!" Julian yelled, running toward the stairs that would lead him up to her.

She couldn't answer; Nazer had her pinned against the glass, the corner of his vest digging into her side.

"You have courage to die fighting," he breathed into her face.

He tried to twist her hand behind her, putting enough pressure on her arm that she cried out in pain. Rallying, she pushed back, using her legs against the glass wall as leverage. Feeling the fractured wall crack even more against the back of her pants, it suddenly became clear what she had to do. They were three floors up, an open-air atrium was right below them, with a concrete floor. Using every last bit of strength she had, she grabbed Nazer's arm and flipped him around so he was against the safety wall, and pushed him, praying the glass would fold under his weight.

For a split second time was suspended. Then the glass gave way behind him. Nazer teetered on the edge, grasping for something to save him, but there was only air. His brow furrowed in confused surprise the moment he knew he was going to fall to the floor below.

"No!" he shouted.

Zaya watched, breathing hard, letting herself feel a moment of satisfaction. Until she saw his thumb press the trigger switch on the vest.

"Julian, incoming!" she screamed, then snatched Hugh in her arms and ran, searching for something solid to hide behind–a pillar, a door—anything for cover.

She ended up behind a pillar as a loud rumble shook the floor enough to knock Zaya to her knees. She managed to hold onto Hugh as smoke and dust floated up to them. Staying down, Zaya waited a moment longer, hoping the building stayed solid beneath her.

Julian! Had he heard her warning? Was he alive?

Hugh was sobbing uncontrollably, pressing his face into her shirtfront. She wanted to get downstairs, to see if Julian was all right, but she needed to calm the boy first. She pressed a kiss to Hugh's forehead.

"It's okay," she murmured. "We're okay."

"I want to go home. I want my mummy," he said over and over. "Please."

"We'll get you home to your mum," she soothed.

"Don't let me go." Hugh tightened his arms around her neck, and Zaya could barely breathe.

She stood awkwardly, keeping him safe against her body. Steeling herself to not react, she limped awkwardly down the first flight of stairs. An airplane that overlooked the third floor was on fire, the flames licking over the cockpit. Zaya pressed Hugh close to her chest. She focused on shielding him as best she could, but as they descended, her steps were unsteady.

Julian had to be alive. With Nazer finally gone, she and Julian deserved a life together, free from him and all his heinous attempts to keep them apart and destroy their lives. They couldn't be separated. Not now.

She stumbled down the second flight of stairs, the smoke getting heavier as a burning plane heaved burning chunks of fuselage to the floor. On the last turn before the stairs that led to the main floor, she paused to readjust Hugh's weight and took a look at the scene in front of them. Her breath caught in her throat. Glass, smoke, and debris covered the entire area, which was lit up by the fiery remnants of several displays.

And there was no sign of Julian anywhere.

CHAPTER TWENTY

The minute Julian heard Zaya scream, he'd run for her, knowing he needed cover, but wanting somehow to get to her. Spying a Soviet tank near the stairs, he took that split second to use its bulk for protection from Nazer's bomb. The explosion was powerful enough to send glass and debris like missiles through the air. A large chunk caught Julian in the head. Blackness overwhelmed him, and he fought unconsciousness, as he fell to the floor.

When he came to, water from the overhead sprinkler system was hitting him in the face, but he was still coughing, the smoke thicker now. Taking stock of his injuries, beyond his head feeling like knives were being stabbed into it, he could feel blood rushing down his arm again, but he couldn't tell if he'd opened his old wound or received a new one.

He tried to sit up, but the pain was excruciating and he propped himself up against the tank. "Is anyone there?" he called into his comms. "Jake? Anyone?"

The Capture

Nothing but static sounded in his ear, so he took it out. The last he'd seen of his team, Colt had stood near Brenna on the far side of the atrium. He rubbed his eyes, trying to see through the smoke, and thought he saw three figures picking their way toward him, leaving a wide berth where Nazer had fallen.

"Julian!" one of them called.

Jake. Relief surged through Julian. They were alive. They'd made it.

"You guys all right?" Julian winced as his own voice sent pain shooting through his skull.

They reached him, sidestepping several hunks of concrete. "We're a little banged up." Colt shook his head, and glass went flying from his hair. "But we're all accounted for."

"What about Zaya?" Brenna asked, when they drew closer. She had her arm around Colt, not putting any weight on her right foot.

"Are you really okay?" Julian asked, watching their progress. Brenna's face was chalk white.

"A chunk of concrete came down on her foot. I think her ankle's broken." Colt drew her closer. "We need to get her to the hospital."

"We need to find Zaya," Brenna protested. "You go on up ahead and get her. I'll be right behind you."

"Stay here, Brenna. Colt, you stay with her while Jake and I go take a look around." Julian leaned heavily on the tank runners as he slowly stood. Dizziness assailed him, but he

238

pushed through it. They couldn't wait a second longer. He turned and stepped over some bits of burning airplane that littered the floor, smoke searing his eyes. He didn't want his last image of Zaya to be watching her trying to fend off Nazer. With his focus on the stairway, trying to keep one foot in front of the other, he moved steadily forward, but his heart was in his throat.

She'd saved them all, but was she okay?

Facing the stairs, he wiped his face, trying to see through the rapidly rising smoke. Putting a hand on the stair rail to stabilize himself, he looked up. There Zaya stood, standing a few steps above him. She descended slowly, holding the little boy in her arms, staring at him as if he were a ghost.

"Julian?" She was coughing, her voice hesitant and uncertain. He nearly leaped up the steps to her.

Hugh wiggled out of her arms just before Julian reached her. She was alive. Courageous. Beautiful. His.

"You're hurt," she murmured as he pulled her into an embrace. There wasn't any better feeling in the world than having her in his arms.

"You're alive," he said, running his hands over her hair, shoulders, and then up to caress her cheeks and jaw. "I was so scared for you." Leaning forward, he touched his lips to hers, a kiss born of need and reassurance. She wrapped her arms around his neck, drawing him closer, breathing him in. He rained kisses along her jaw to her ear. "You're amazing," he whispered to her.

"Can I go home now?" Hugh asked plaintively. "It's getting smoky."

Zaya wiped tears from her face and laughed. Reaching for Hugh's hand, she took it. "Let's all go home."

They went down the rest of the stairs slowly, met at the bottom by the rest of the team.

"I'm glad to see you made it in one piece," Brenna said, giving her soot-covered jeans and t-shirt a once-over as Zaya moved to her side. "But we need to find you another change of clothes."

"That's almost becoming a full time job for you, isn't it?" Zaya said with a smile.

"I don't mind. We're a similar size, so I shop for myself at the same time." They started slowly toward the door, pausing to wait for Brenna, but they all stopped for a moment to look at the spot where the bomb had gone off. With an explosion that size, there wouldn't be anything left of Nazer. He was gone from all of their lives now, but the effects of his presence would be felt for years to come. It was a sobering moment for Julian.

He slipped an arm around Zaya, not only to have her close, but to steady himself. He'd had concussions before, but he didn't want to be weak right now. With one last glance at the fire and smoke, a realization bolted through him. His hunt for Nazer was really over. The focus of his life for so long—ending Nazer's ability to hurt and terrorize people, while bringing down his organization—had finally happened.

Sirens wailed beyond the doors, and when Julian led the group through the front, he wasn't surprised to see every sort of emergency vehicle possible waiting. There was also a fair number of government vehicles, which made sense with someone as high profile as Nazer being involved. Wiping a hand across his face, Julian kept them moving. They all needed to see a doctor, then take a much-deserved vacation.

As if Elliott had heard his wish, he nearly sprinted across the grass toward them. "Everyone o-okay?"

"Brenna needs some attention," Colt said, immediately. "Ankle's broken, I think."

A paramedic joined Elliott, and they took Brenna and Colt to another area, close to an ambulance. Zaya sat on the ground where she stood, exhausted. She kept Hugh close, rubbing his back, providing some comfort. Physically, neither of them seemed hurt, but Julian knew emotionally, both of them could have long-lasting wounds.

He sat next to them, his body grateful for the reprieve, watching as the paramedics examined Brenna and Colt. Elliott broke from the group and came over to Julian. "L-looks like you could use s-some attention, too," he remarked.

Julian looked down at his arm. Blood had soaked his shirt and body armor, but with everything going on, he hadn't really felt it. Stinging pain was starting to make its way up his shoulder, though, meshing with the ache in his head, and he grimaced. "Yeah, I think I ripped my stitches."

Elliott touched the side of his head. "And f-from the l-look of things, you took a pretty h-hard hit to the head."

He bent and opened his bag to get supplies to clean the wound. Zaya merely watched, her expression unreadable. What

241

was she thinking? Was she just overwhelmed, coming down off of an adrenaline rush or did her silence mean something else was going on?

He didn't have time to analyze it further before a woman's screamed, "Hugh!"

Caroline Alden sprinted across the grass, dodging anyone who stood in her way. Hugh stood and started walking toward her, but didn't make it far before his mother snatched him up and hugged him tightly to her chest.

"Hugh," she said over and over, in between kissing his hair and face.

Hugh was crying so hard, he buried his face in her neck. "Mummy, I was so scared," he choked out.

"You're safe now. I'll never let anything happen to you," his mother reassured him. She tilted her head so she could see Zaya. "Thank you. I know if it weren't for you I might not have seen him again."

"Hugh is a very brave boy," she told them, standing slowly and touching Hugh's shoulder. "Always remember that, okay, little man?"

"Okay," he said, before nestling into his mother's arms again.

A paramedic made his way over to them, putting on some medical gloves. "Ma'am, I'd like to check your son for any injuries. Will you follow me?"

Caroline nodded, but let the paramedic take a few steps away. "Thank you," she said to Zaya again. "I can never repay you."

"I was glad to help. It . . . put some things in perspective for me so I can sleep at night." Her cheeks flushed a little, as if she was debating her next words. "Nazer gave me nightmares."

"He had that effect on a lot of people." Caroline reached out and touched Zaya's shoulder. "If you ever want to talk, I'm available. We might have a few things in common."

"I'd like that." Zaya smiled, and Julian could see the light in her eyes. Shadows were still lurking there somewhere, but the suffocating blackness from before seemed to have been banished by the light. The band of worry that weighed so heavily on him evaporated. She was going to be all right. *They* were going to be all right.

Elliott had cut away his sleeve, and his intake of breath made Julian look away from Zaya and down at his arm. "What's wrong?"

"You've got g-glass shards and little bits of m-metal embedded in your arm around the g-gunshot wound I sewed up earlier. You're g-going to need to be in the hospital to make sure they g-get them all out properly. I don't w-want to see this g-get infected." Elliott glanced over at Zaya. "Wh-what about you? Any injuries I should know about?"

She held up her arm that was swelling and discolored. "In that last scuffle with Nazer, I think he broke my wrist." She swayed a little and Elliott quickly moved to her side.

The Capture

"Why didn't you say anything?" Julian murmured. She'd been hurt all this time– and holding a small boy on a possibly broken wrist. He should have noticed.

"Same reason you didn't, I guess," she grimaced and held her injured wrist. "Adrenaline is a powerful thing."

"Let's get you to a hospital," he said. He stood, his whole body feeling as if he'd been run over by a tank. What a pair they made. "How's your foot?"

"I'll live." She limped a few steps away from him to follow Elliott toward the line of ambulances, but Julian lightly held her good arm.

"Are you okay? Really?" he asked, his eyes full of concern. "I know what you've been through today will give you that much more to work through."

She looked up at him, her brown eyes serious and troubled. "I had moments of panic, I won't deny that. And there are some things I want to talk over with Dr. Finch, but overall, I feel like I've been given a second chance. I didn't let the darkness win."

Julian felt tears pricking the back of his throat. "I always knew you were a warrior."

She wiped away an escaping tear of her own, but curved her lips into a smile. "I knew you were coming for me. That helped."

He thought of the moments where they hadn't been sure they would find her and once again felt relief that they had– and in time. "You gave us great clues and did all the work."

She pressed into his side. "We did it together."

They followed in Elliott's footsteps when a man in a dark suit approached them, blocking the path.

"Ms. Altes. Commander Bennet." He nodded to both of them. "I don't know if you remember me . . ."

"Harry Barton, right?" Julian said, reaching out to shake his hand. "I remember William mentioning that you'd been promoted to Assistant Director awhile back."

"Yes, well, I'd like to talk to you about Chief Sinclair." He looked at Zaya, an apology on his face. "I know this is a bad time, but we've been to the house in Surrey where you're staying, and we have a few questions." He waved a hand at the museum behind them. "And obviously, we need your statements about what happened inside."

Julian let his shoulders drop, fatigue and pain finally hitting him hard. "We're on our way to the hospital. Can we put this off for a few days? We'll still help in any way we can." His mind went to William's last moments. "And I'd like to talk to Chief Sinclair's widow myself, if I could. As a professional courtesy." He needed to explain things to her, and make sure she knew that William died a hero.

Harry gave him a wide-eyed look, glancing down at his bloody clothing. It was obvious he didn't think Julian was anywhere near presentable to talk to William's widow. "Were you planning to see her personally?"

"Don't worry, I'll clean up. But William had some last words he wanted me to give her, and I want to do that for him."

And he wanted to assure Amelia that her husband would always be remembered as a good man who lived an extraordinary life.

"As the acting head of MI6, that's my duty to perform," Harry said apologetically, running a hand down his tie.

Julian was about to protest. He didn't want this to become a "who-has-more-authority" kind of thing, but then Harry held up a hand.

"Knowing how close you were to William, I'll give you that. Just let me know when you're going. I'd like to go with you, at least." He looked Julian in the eye. "If that's acceptable?"

"It is, thank you." They all turned and walked toward the ambulances. "Did you secure Atwah?"

"Yes. Thanks to your intel, he was never moved. The pilots scrambled from RAF Benson took care of Nazer's helicopter. The pilot was arrested and several other men on the ground, as well." Just before they reached the first ambulance, Harry turned. "I wanted to say that I know Aldworth resented you for Griffin Force's success and thought you were in it to make MI6 look expendable. Hopefully in the next few months we'll get some idea of what motivated him to go so far as to betray his country."

"I'd like to see those reports, if you don't mind," Julian said, but there was a good chance they'd never know what could radicalize a man like that.

"Of course. From the files I've read and from what Chief Sinclair has said, you are doing a great thing with Griffin Force."

Harry stopped a few yards away from the ambulance. "I hope we'll be able to work together in the future."

"I'll definitely be in touch," Julian said as he squared his shoulders. He needed to sit down. Soon.

"Here's my card." Harry gave it to him, then paused for a moment before reaching out to shake Julian's hand. "People around the world will be thanking your team for everything you did today." Julian nodded and they all watched Harry join a small crowd of men dressed similarly.

If he ends up being the new head of MI6, he'll be a good one. Julian could already see a partnership of sorts forming between him and Harry, as it had with William. But now that Nazer was gone, would he continue Griffin Force? Disband it? Give it to Colt? There were so many things to think about.

"Your wrist may need surgery," he said quietly to Zaya.

"Your head needs to be looked at, and your arm as well," she murmured. "Do you think we can get hospital rooms next to each other so I can keep an eye on you? Trouble seems to follow you around."

He chuckled at her attempt to lighten the mood and put his good arm around her. "I think you have that backwards." Easily turning her into his embrace, he stared down at her familiar brown eyes. "Have I told you how amazing you are?" He kissed her softly. "And how much I love you?"

Reaching up, she kissed him back, touching her thumb to the indent in his chin. "As long as you remember I said it first."

The Capture

"I may have a concussion, but I definitely remember that I said it first, about eight months ago." He raised an eyebrow. "Remember?"

"But if we're starting over, that one was void." She tucked her head against his chest. "Maybe we can just call it a draw."

"Ooh, I like it when you talk in sports analogies. How about a replay?" He kissed her again, a quick peck on the lips. "Or my personal favorite, slow-motion?" He leaned down, his eyes on her lips as his thumb ran over her jawline. Millimeter by millimeter he watched her reaction, grinning at the impatient look in her eyes. Finally she went up on her tiptoes and closed the distance between them, kissing him soundly.

"Three minutes in the penalty box?" she murmured.

"I like how you think," he said with a laugh, before he bent his head to hers again. "Let me show you how I'll spend my three minutes."

He kissed her deeply this time, savoring their connection. His hands tangled in her hair, and for a moment the chaos behind them melted away, reaffirming everything he'd always known. They were meant to be together. While they'd walked through fire to get to this point, and there were likely to be more bumps along the way, they'd face it all together.

And he knew they'd be brilliant at it.

CHAPTER TWENTY-ONE

Zaya pushed open the hospital room door and wasn't surprised to see Julian sitting on the side of his bed, dressed and ready to go. He'd hated every minute of being here, but his wounds and concussion had needed an extra couple of days of observation and healing. She'd been discharged yesterday, with a cast on her wrist and strict instructions to take it easy.

"I'm here to help you escape," she said with a smile.

He stood and crossed the room to pull her close. "My deliverer. I thought you'd never get here. How are you feeling?"

"Good." She slid her arms around his neck and pressed her lips to his, lingering longer than she should have, but unable to resist. "I got here as fast as I could."

A throat-clearing behind them interrupted. "Commander Bennet, I just have a few more papers for you to sign before you're discharged." The pretty young nurse handed him a clipboard. "Also, here are some of your personal effects. Your watch, ring, and chain."

The Capture

Zaya took the small bag from her, surprised. "I've never known you to wear jewelry before."

Julian reached for the bag, but Zaya pulled it out of his reach. "Z, it's not . . . I don't want . . ."

But she already had the bag open and was pulling out a silver chain with a beautiful emerald ring dangling from it. Immediately, she knew it was the engagement ring he'd bought the day she'd been abducted. She held it out. "I'm sorry."

The awkwardness in the room multiplied as he stood there, looking at her hand with the ring in it.

"I'll just stop by in a few minutes to pick up those papers," the nurse said, before she exited the room.

Julian stared at the ring and didn't reach out to take it. "What are you sorry for? That ring was supposed to be something special, but it ended up being bad luck."

Zaya pulled it back and turned it over, looking at the beautiful green stone, surrounded by tiny diamonds. "Do you know why I love emeralds so much?"

Julian finally looked up and met her eyes, his brows furrowed. "No, I don't think so."

"My grandmother had these beautiful emerald earrings and a matching bracelet. When my parents died and I went to live with her, I was a mess. Never slept, and I cried a lot. My grandma would spend hours singing me lullabies and walking with me. Walking is good for the soul, she said. But no matter if she was wearing a housedress or a Sunday dress, she always wore her emerald bracelet and earrings."

Julian sat on the edge of the hospital bed and gently tugged her down with him. "Was green her favorite color?"

"Probably. But she told me that emeralds symbolized hope in the future, and they had an energy around them that provided healing. So when my parents died, she wore them all the time to heal her heart and remember that there was always hope." Zaya looked down at the ring in her hand. "She gave me her emerald bracelet to wear every day so I could have the same things in my heart. And wouldn't you know it, I started sleeping and didn't feel like crying as much. I've loved emeralds ever since."

He took her hand in his, letting the chain fall over their intertwined fingers. "The jeweler in Morocco told me that emeralds were a symbol of renewal, but I didn't think much of it at the time. I wanted that ring to represent us, our love, and the happiness we'd found together."

"It still can. When we're ready." She looked up at him with a tender smile. "I know I have a long way to go still, to truly figure out what my new normal is and how that will fit with our relationship. But I can't imagine my life without you in it."

"We've already made a good start toward our new normal," he said, kissing her temple.

"Exactly." She closed her hand around the ring. "Maybe I could wear this around my neck, just to keep it close to my heart until we're ready to put it on my finger."

"An excellent idea." He took the chain from her and slipped it around her neck with a kiss. "I love you."

"I love you back, but we'll see how long those feelings last during your recuperation. I've heard you can be a stubborn and beastly patient." She laughed at his wide eyes and look of mock offense. "Don't try to deny it."

"I'll deny it until my last breath. I am a *model* patient." He leaned his elbow on one knee. "Perhaps it's the ghastly food that made me cranky."

Standing, she went to the rollaway table and handed him the discharge papers. "You won't have that excuse at your parents' house. They're expecting us, and they've invited me to stay to help while you convalesce."

Julian's playful expression immediately turned into a scowl. "I don't need to 'convalesce' at all. I'm fine."

"The doctor recommended that you take a few days to let your body thoroughly heal. I agree with that assessment, and so do your parents." She came closer and ran her hand through his hair, careful of the stitches on the side of his head. "Just think, long walks through the woods, evenings with Milo and me by the fire."

He leaned in, his hand curving around her waist. "Well, when you put it that way, convalescing doesn't sound so bad. We can do it together."

"Will you be able to get away from all your Griffin Force duties?" His touch was giving her butterflies. She was more than ready to start their retreat from the world and didn't want him to have any distractions.

"Actually, I was going to talk to you about that." He pulled away to look at her. "I've been thinking a lot about what you said that day, that I could walk away from it all. I think I'm going to turn Griffin Force over to Colt, but stay on as a consultant." He tilted his head, as if trying to gauge her reaction. "It seems like the right thing to do, and Colt likes the idea. We've already been in close contact with Harry getting all the preliminaries taken care of, and finalizing the details of Nazer's case."

Even the mention of the terrorist's name still jolted Zaya, but she noticed that those visceral reactions were starting to fade. "Anything new?"

"No. It's an open and shut suicide bombing." He stood and put his arm around her shoulders. "With the strength of that bomb, though, I'm forever grateful we all made it out in one piece."

"Well, most of us did," Brenna said from the doorway, hobbling in on her crutches. "My ankle has a few new pieces of metal holding it together."

The rest of the team crowded in behind her. "How are you feeling?" Jake asked. "Glad to be going home?"

Julian smiled at them, like a benevolent older brother. "Definitely. I know Colt talked to you this morning about the possible change, but when it happens, don't think I won't be checking in on you guys from time to time. I'm still a consultant for the team, and you can come to me anytime," Julian said, meeting each team member's eyes. "But other than that, I'm going to be at home, eating good food and catching up on lost time with Zaya."

Colt rubbed his chin. "Sounds like it will be hard to tear you away from retirement, but I hope you'll come back into London for the wedding." Colt held up Brenna's hand, where a diamond sparkled from her ring finger. "We're getting married."

The room erupted in congratulations as they all moved forward to hug the happy couple. "With Mya and Jake's wedding coming up, the only people not married on the task force will be Augie, Nate, and Elliott." Julian lifted his eyebrows. "We may have to help you blokes along."

Elliott held up his hands. "I've got this c-covered on my end. I'm seeing Charlie again t-tonight."

Jake elbowed him. "Isn't that the third time this week?"

"Sure is." Elliott grinned. "And if I g-get my way, I'll see h-her *every* night this week and whenever else she'll agree to s-see me." Everyone laughed along with him.

"Of course we'll all be there for the wedding," Julian said, squeezing Zaya's shoulders. "Wouldn't miss it for the world. After everything we've been through, we're family."

When Colt's phone rang, the good mood dissipated. He looked at Brenna apologetically. "I have to take this." He moved to the doorway, stepping just outside of the room before he said hello.

The entire team grew quiet, shamelessly eavesdropping. "When?" Colt asked, his tone stunned. There was silence for a moment, before Colt said, "We'll be right there."

Colt walked back into the room, not surprised to see them all watching him. "I guess you heard that?" he held up his phone.

"What's going on?" Julian asked.

"Belmarsh is in lockdown. Atwah is missing." He shook his head. "He was in a high-security area. There shouldn't have been anywhere for him to go."

"They want backup?" Jake asked, already heading for the door. "I'm sure the entire intelligence community has been mobilized."

Zaya laid her hand on Julian's arm, a sliver of the old darkness threading through her veins. "Could this have anything to do with Nazer? His final plan to break Atwah out?"

"I don't know, but the sooner we find him, the easier I'll sleep tonight. I'll call you later," Colt promised as the team filed out the door.

"Get well," Brenna told Julian before she left. "We'll be down to visit and let you know all the details of the wedding."

When the room was empty except for the two of them, Zaya put her head on Julian's shoulder. "Do you want to go with them? See this through?" Part of her wanted him on the mission because he was the best, but the other part wanted him safe at her side.

"No." He held his hand over hers. "I'll be available if they need to consult with me, but I trust them. I'm starting a new chapter of my life today."

The Capture

Zaya's chest rose and fell with a deep breath. "Are you sure?"

"Definitely." His eyes were full of promise as they looked into hers, her future filled with light, happiness, and love—everything that Zaya had longed for. He pulled her close, their lips brushing in a light kiss before he put his forehead to hers. "The things we've done, been through, and witnessed are a part of us. But I think we can fight the darkness if it starts to creep in as long as we're together."

"It's going to take a lot of communication. Dr. Finch will probably have us writing in our journals, talking about our emotions, and working on our breathing. All of your favorite things. Can you handle that?" she asked with a grin, his fingers combing through her hair and sending shivers down her spine.

"I'll talk, write, and even draw pictures for you if that's what it takes." His hands were going down her back, a light pressure inching her closer.

"I love you," she said, letting her own hands explore the stubble on his jaw and the shape of his face. He'd never given up on them and the strength of their love had kept her alive, even during the darkest days. He was part of her and always would be. "So much."

He lowered his lips to hers, their mouths meeting in a kiss as powerful as the words they'd just spoken to each other.

And though her home had changed in the months she'd been missing, in that moment Zaya knew her heart and soul were finally where they belonged.

ABOUT THE AUTHOR

Julie Coulter Bellon is an award-winning author of nearly two dozen published books. She loves to travel and her favorite cities she's visited so far are probably Athens, Paris, Ottawa, and London. She would love to visit Hawaii, Australia, Ireland, and Scotland someday. She also loves to read, write, teach, watch Hawaii Five-O, and eat Canadian chocolate. Not necessarily in that order.

Julie offers writing and publishing tips, as well as her take on life on her blog http://ldswritermom.blogspot.com/ You can also find out about all her upcoming projects at her website www.juliebellon.com or you can follow her on Twitter @juliebellon

Made in the USA
Columbia, SC
09 December 2019